RICK SHANNON AND THE CASE OF THE MISSING PILOT

Rick Shannon

AND THE CASE OF THE MISSING PILOT

ALLAN STEWART

WindRider BOOKS

Tyndale House Publishers, Inc., Wheaton, Illinois

First printing, January 1985
ISBN 0-8423-0212-3, paper
Printed in the United States of America

CONTENTS

ONE
MOUNTAIN VALLEY CRASH

The helicopter came into the valley out of the blinding sunlight, and dropped into the cool blue shadow cast by the mountain.

In the front passenger seat, Rick Shannon leaned forward to peer intently through the plexiglass.

Somewhere up in this maze of peaks, ridges, canyons and valleys that they called the Sierra Nevada, a Cessna 172 was down. Two days ago, on Saturday afternoon, the small plane had left White Valley, California, for a routine flight across the mountains to Nevada.

It had never arrived.

A flash of reflected sunlight caught Rick's attention. A second helicopter was sliding over the ridge to the north. Five thousand feet above it a twin-engined Beechcraft drew a circle between the peaks.

This was the place, Rick thought. This had to be the valley they were looking for. It fit the description they had been given.

A hiker with a CB unit in his backpack had given them their first clue to finding the missing plane. He said he had spotted the wreck through binoculars from the shoulder of a mountain to the northwest. A fire lookout tower up near Sonora Pass had picked up his signal and relayed it to the search planes.

That's why they were now hovering over this tight, granite-walled valley.

"See anything?" Marc Blair, the pilot, pushed a strand of blond hair away from his eyes, then adjusted his headset. He let the Bell Jet Ranger sink a little lower.

"Nothing," Rick said. He squeezed his eyes shut tight as the helicopter lurched and wobbled on the unpredictable air currents surging in and out of the valley.

It had been like that since early morning. Ten hours of lurching, bucking, twisting, and sliding, interrupted only by refueling stops. The helicopter had been riding the air turbulence in the high Sierras like a champion rodeo bronc trying to unseat its rider.

If that feeling in his stomach was anything to go by, Rick thought it just might succeed. He was ready to get out and walk—anytime.

They dropped a few more feet. With the gentle pressure of the pilot's left foot on the rudder pedal, the helicopter did a slow pivot in the center of the valley.

Nothing but rocks and trees.

Another time around.

Still nothing.

Rick leaned back and stretched his six-foot frame, then rubbed his eyes. Ten hours of staring intensely at rocky hillsides made them burn with fatigue. It was difficult to focus clearly, but he forced himself to concentrate his gaze along the east wall of the valley, straining to pick out details that made some kind of sense.

He'd lost count of how many times they had dived to take a closer look at a bleached tree trunk or a strangely shaped rock outcropping that from a distance looked vaguely like it might be a plane.

For Rick, the day had started out normally enough—if his routine could be called normal. He had a picture taking assignment for Starr News Features. Nothing special. The pictures he took weren't likely to end up in anyone's scrapbook. They'd be printed in some magazine or news-paper—down in the bottom corner—and then filed away in some deep, dark, and forgotten file drawer.

At first, working for an international news and photo agency like Starr had sounded like some-thing special. When he was offered the new job at the end of his trip to Florida earlier in the summer, he had dreams of traveling on assign-ment to exotic, faraway places. So far his longest, most exotic trip had been to a dusty town about a hundred miles away. His assignment schedule had been packed so full that he had spent nearly half his time helping out at his uncle's newspaper, the White Valley Gazette. He'd even managed a couple of afternoons a week working at Shannon Electronics.

Today a newsmagazine in New York wanted a picture of a flood-control dam being constructed somewhere up in the mountains east of Sacra-mento. Just one picture to fill a small space in a story they were doing. The magazine had called Starr News. The assignment man at Starr had called Rick. And almost before he knew it he was in a chartered helicopter heading for the mountains.

For a moment or two Rick had thought that maybe this time it would be different. An aerial shot from a helicopter certainly sounded dramatic. But his instructions over the phone erased that fleeting thought in short order: "Don't do anything tricky. Don't be creative. Just give them a picture that sets the scene, and shows the information they want. Nothing more."

That's the way it had started. And if it hadn't been for the emergency radio message that came through less than twenty minutes after they lifted off from White Valley airport, he'd have been back on solid ground long before lunchtime.

A few terse words on the radio had quickly turned his assignment into a very different kind of story—a grim life-and-death search that, at last count, included eighteen planes and three helicopters.

"There she is!"

Rick's thoughts snapped back into high gear.

There was no doubt about it this time. This was no rock outcropping or bleached tree trunk.

A long line of broken treetops told the dramatic story of the Cessna's last few moments. At the end of that line, an orange, blue, and white shape sprawled on the talus slope near the foot of a long cliff. Twisted and battered, it looked like a broken toy discarded by a child.

With a few quick words into his microphone, Marc passed the news to the plane circling above them.

Orange, blue, and white. . . . There was something familiar about those colors, Rick thought. Then as the helicopter slipped sideways a dozen feet, the neat black lettering on the door of the plane seemed to jump out at him: BLAIR AVIATION.

Of course! The same broad bands of color were painted on the helicopter.

Rick turned abruptly. Marc Blair nodded, his face grim. "It's one of ours."

"But you didn't say—"

"I know," Marc said. "I should have told you."

"Why . . . ?"

Marc shrugged. "I suppose I didn't want to admit that it was really possible. A lot of small planes fly this route. There was a chance that it wasn't—" He broke off. "Crazy, huh?"

"I don't think so," Rick murmured. His fingers twisted the Nikon's lens quickly to bring the crash scene into focus. It wouldn't be a prizewinning picture, but it sure set the scene. "Your father's company?"

"No. Cousin." The pilot's lips tightened as his eyes probed the tangled, battered wreckage below them. "The company has been running charters and rentals for ten years. Maybe more. In all that time, we've never lost a plane—until today. Never even had a serious accident. Now he . . . I. . . ." Marc stumbled over the words as his voice skidded to a stop.

Rick watched him, waiting for the pilot to continue.

Marc took a breath. "Forget it."

Rick's eyebrows raised with an unspoken question. Marc was troubled. That was easy to tell. He had reason to be. That plane down there was from Blair Aviation. But was it only worry? Rick wondered. Or did the tension in Marc's voice mean that he was feeling something more than a normal concern over the wrecked plane? The pilot's white-knuckled grip of the controls said that maybe there was. But one glance told him that Marc wasn't about to share his feelings.

"Who's the pilot?"

Marc studied the wreck as his shoulders lifted in a shrug. "Don't know. Never saw him. I wasn't working when he picked up the plane. One of the other guys signed it out."

Rick frowned. Why did Marc sound so defensive? Or was he reading too much into those few brief words? He remembered his father telling him once—after a long day attempting to track down some missing computer parts at Shannon Electronics—that a tired mind and an overactive imagination were a bad combination. Maybe this was one of those times. He certainly was plenty tired.

"I can't land anywhere close." Marc's voice cut in on his thoughts. "No level ground." He suddenly sounded very sharp and businesslike again. He nodded toward an open stretch of rocky slope at the foot of the cliff. "I'll touch down over there and you'll have to jump for it."

"Right," Rick agreed. He eyed the scattered chunks of jagged granite. "I don't suppose you could find me a soft spot."

A faint smile flickered across the pilot's face.

For a brief instant the worry lines softened.

Rick swung his camera over his shoulder, and stuffed a compact walkie-talkie into a jacket pocket.

He shot another quick glance toward the wreck as Marc edged the helicopter close to the slope. One thing was certain. This wouldn't be one of those storybook accidents that ended with the pilot climbing out and walking away with a slight limp. The very least they could expect would be a serious injury.

They touched ground with a gentle bump. Rick slid across the seat toward the door. "I'll let you know as soon as I take a look," he said, patting the walkie-talkie.

Marc nodded.

The radio squawked before Rick could say anything further.

Marc replied briefly into his microphone, listened to another half dozen quick words, and then told Rick, "Better hurry it up. The others are coming in now. You'll have company in just about two minutes."

Rick nodded as he swung through the door and dropped to the ground. Before he could scramble to his feet again, the Bell Jet Ranger was pulling up and away to make room for the second helicopter. Above the roar of the two machines he could hear the heavy *thump-thump* motor sound of a third helicopter—a big eight-seater—coming into the valley.

Rick eyed the battered little plane as he picked his way across the slope, and couldn't help the low pitched whistle that escaped from his lips. From close by it looked even worse than it had from up above. There wasn't much left except the badly battered body and tail section. The propeller was gone. So was the landing gear. But that was to be expected. The wings were missing, too. They had probably ripped off as the Cessna bounced and crashed through the tops of the trees, before it finally came to rest, nose up, on the rocky hillside.

It had been a rough ride, those last few seconds.

At least there was one good thing to report, Rick noted. There was no sign of fire or smoke. Was that unusual? Or was it only on television that cars and planes and boats exploded into great balls of orange flame when they crashed?

A moment later he forgot the thought of fire as he pulled himself up level with the cockpit window and peered inside.

The plane was empty.

There was no pilot.

T W O
STRANGE PUZZLE

Impossible!

It was the first word to explode in Rick's mind as he stared into the empty cockpit. There was no way the pilot could have walked away from the tangled mess that used to be a plane. No one could have come out of that crash with anything less than a serious injury. Broken bones, at least. And anyone seriously injured would still be inside.

But when Rick moved to one side for a better angle, the result was the same. There was no one in the plane.

But that couldn't be.

He spun around and scanned the ground on all sides of the wreck. But there was nothing to be seen on the open slope except rocks, and sticks, and scattered small shrubs.

A frown creased Rick's face as he reached for the handle of the door and pulled on it.

It didn't budge.

Again.

Still nothing.

If the pilot had somehow managed to survive the crash and leave the plane, he certainly hadn't done it by way of either of the doors. Not with one of them firmly jammed in place and the other blocked by a solid slab of mountain granite. One glance quickly eliminated the windows as possibilities. They were cracked and broken, all right. But none of the holes was big enough for a man to crawl through.

He must still be inside then, Rick thought. But there was no trace of him.

Rick looked through the window at the instrument panel. Most of the indicators were still intact. The fuel gauge still hung near the halfway mark. Was that possible? Could the fuel tank have somehow survived the impact of the crash? Was that why the plane hadn't burned?

Rick sniffed. There was no sign of fumes.

There had been no emergency messages either. No calls for help from a plane in trouble. Only that brief CB message saying that a hiker had seen what he thought might be the wreck of a plane.

Rick eyed the fuel gauge again, thoughtfully. It could be stuck. On the other hand, if the reading was correct, if there was still fuel in the tank, what had caused the little Cessna to crash?

There could be a number of different explanations. Engine trouble. A fouled spark plug. Or perhaps the pilot had suddenly become sick or unconscious. It happened once in awhile to people in cars, so why not in a plane? But, if that had happened, the pilot would still be in the plane.

"Impossible!" he said aloud, pulling the walkie-talkie from his pocket. It was the only word he could think of to describe the situation.

Marc Blair's reaction a moment later, when Rick gave him the news, was an echo of his own.

Rick let the radio hang limply at his side. He looked toward the top of the cliff where Marc had landed. Rick could imagine the look of disbelief on the pilot's face.

Within less than ten minutes six men had dropped to the ground from the other two helicopters. They hurried expectantly to the wreck and were bewildered by the empty cockpit.

Rick stood back and watched as they scrambled over the rocks and circled what was left of the little plane. Not satisfied by anyone else's results, each of them had to examine it for himself from every possible angle. They peered through the cracked and broken windows. They scanned every inch of the cockpit and the four empty seats. And they grunted and muttered to themselves as they pulled and tugged on the door. Each of them had to try it to be sure.

In the end they each came to the same conclusion. The plane was empty and the battered doors could not be opened.

The opinion was unanimous. There was no way anyone could have left the plane after the impact of the crash.

Where, then, was the pilot? If he wasn't in the plane or on the ground nearby, where was he?

After a moment of discussion, four of the men went into the woods, backtracking beneath the trail of broken treetops. They were spread well apart to cover ground on both sides of the trail. They looked for pieces of wreckage and anything else that might tell them a part of the story.

There was just one slender thread of hope left.

An unspoken idea that Rick knew each man was thinking. Perhaps—just perhaps—the pilot had somehow been thrown clear when the plane first hit the trees. He'd be in bad shape if he survived the fall, but he might still be back there. It wasn't much on which to hang their hopes. But it was enough to keep them looking a little longer.

When they returned an hour later, though, words were hardly necessary. Their faces said enough. They'd found more of the wreckage—parts of the wings, propeller, and landing gear. But that was all.

There was no sign of the pilot. Not even a scrap of clothing.

Instinctively Rick took a quick series of pictures of the returning men. The zoom lens reached out and brought them in close, so that each detail was dramatically clear in the viewfinder—their grim expressions, the tightly pressed lips. As often as he had used that lens and seen that same effect, it still gave him a strange feeling. It was almost as though the lens allowed him to step inside their minds to feel their emotions.

"Who's he?"

The voice sliced into Rick's thoughts.

A fifth man had appeared at the edge of the woods a few steps behind the returning searchers. He was limping, leaning on a forked branch as a makeshift crutch.

One of the four men who had just returned glanced over his shoulder, and shrugged. "Hiker," he said. "The hills are full of them this time of year. We found him a short distance down the valley. Said he sprained his ankle. Asked if he could hitch a ride back with us." He waved a hand toward the pilotless plane. "Under the circumstances, we've got plenty of room."

Rick's quick glance at the newcomer took in the well-worn boots, jeans, and nylon backpack. A good quality 35mm camera hung from his shoulder by a wide, practical, dark-green fabric strap. He was about a day or two away from his last shave. About right for someone who was spending a few days roughing it in the mountains. He looked like what he said he was—a hiker.

For just a second he wondered if this could have been the same hiker who had directed the search team to the wreck. But he quickly dismissed the idea as unlikely.

"You come from the north?" one of the men asked.

The newcomer waved vaguely in the opposite direction. "Southeast. Before that I worked my way up out of Yosemite. Been on the trail about a week."

Rick nodded to himself. What he had described was certainly possible. A year or two back he'd done some hiking in the same area with his father. They'd spent a couple of days on a short stretch of the Pacific Crest Trail. Likely this hiker had been over the same section.

Another man from the search team looked up at the cliff, a thoughtful expression narrowing his eyes. "What'd you do? Fly down?"

"Just about." A faint grin touched the hiker's face. "There's sort of a trail about a half mile back," he explained. "It's steep. But it's passable if you take it easy." He gestured with his free hand. "I wasn't sure I could make it down here before you guys left again. Or that you'd have room for an extra passenger. But I had to take a chance. The nearest road is a long hike out of here. Maybe two or three days with this ankle." He glanced curiously, almost casually at the wreck. "Pretty bad, huh?"

"Pretty bad," someone agreed.

"Need any help?" The hiker looked down at his leg. "Can't do much with this, but—"

"We can manage."

Rick let his mind drift away from their conversation as he climbed a short distance higher up the slope looking for a different angle for another picture. The helicopters would be coming back soon. One or two more pictures would just about wrap it up. Besides, two shots would finish the only film he had brought with him. Like an idiot he had forgotten to stuff extras in his pocket. That was an amateur's trick. Having spare film on hand was a necessary and automatic precaution for every professional photographer. And according to the press card Starr News had sent him, he was supposed to be a professional. Some professional!

Rick took his picture, then thoughtfully eyed the wreck once more. One more face would make the scene complete. But whose face was it? Who was the pilot whose face was the missing ingredient in this picture? What had happened to him? And where was he?

He looked up.

There was little that any of them could do here, now. There was certainly no one to be rescued. There was no need for the stretcher, or the emergency medical supplies that had been unloaded from the big helicopter. All that remained was a puzzle for the government crash investigators who would likely be out first thing in the morning.

Rick looked up as the rhythmic thumping sound suddenly filled the valley again. The helicopters were coming back with Blair Aviation's Jet Ranger in the lead. He could see Marc peering down through the plexiglass.

With a last glance at the battered plane, Rick started down the slope to meet him.

By the direct route, and without any more diving detours into valleys and canyons, the flight back to White Valley took only forty minutes. For most of that trip, Marc Blair was silent. One syllable at a time was about all he would offer.

After a half dozen attempts, Rick gave up. He really couldn't blame Marc for not wanting to talk. There had been a serious accident back there, and Marc's interest and concern went far deeper than that of a casual spectator. There was something personal there. That was obvious. So, why should he open himself up, and share his worry with a stranger?

"Anything I can do?" Rick asked softly.

Marc's answer was a wordless, tight-lipped shake of his head.

If Walter Shannon, Rick's father, had been there, it might have been a different story. Or his uncle, Brett Shannon, the editor of the Gazette. Both of them seemed to have a knack for talking to people and getting them to open up and talk back. The right words came easily to them. They even taught "sharing" classes at the church. It was a talent or gift that ran strong in the Shannon clan. Just like red hair, the trademark of a Shannon for everyone in the family except him—he had dark brown hair. The talking gift was there, too, for everyone but him. He'd watched them in action. But as much as he tried to follow their example, it never seemed to work for him. Once he got to know a person it came easier. But until then. . . .

Maybe that's why he was a photographer and not a reporter, he thought. He could remember vividly how quickly his first summer job with the Gazette had headed for a disaster—until he got his hands on a camera. That's when he discovered he really wasn't cut out to be a reporter. As a photographer he could let his pictures do the talking.

An hour after landing Rick was in the Gazette darkroom, his film processing almost finished, when the telephone loudly demanded his attention.

It was Marc.

"Got that name you wanted," he said. His voice was flat, with little color or expression. "The pilot of the plane. He was—is James Garrett."

Rick made a note. "How about an address?"

"Nothing. Only a box number. The police, I guess, are checking that out."

"What about his destination?"

"Some place over in Nevada, I think."

"You think?" Rick exclaimed. "You don't know where he was going? You don't know where he was taking your plane? Or why?"

"No."

"Isn't that a little strange?"

"Renting a plane is like renting a car," Marc told him. "You sign your name, pay your deposit, and take off. If you have a credit card, that covers it. This guy had a card."

"And that's all there is to it?"

"That's all."

"No flight plan?"

"Nothing like that."

"But I thought—"

"This is a small private field," Marc cut in. "We don't even have a control tower. Not enough traffic." There was a pause as though Marc was chewing over some thought. "How are the pictures?"

Rick leaned over to examine the strip of film. "Look OK, I guess," he answered. "I'll know better in a few minutes when I print them up. Why? You want copies?"

"I suppose," Marc said. He didn't sound especially enthusiastic about the idea.

"I'll print some up for you," Rick said. "Maybe your cousin could use them for the insurance people or something."

"Sure."

Another pause.

"Someone called here about you," Marc said. "About ten minutes ago."

"Yeah?" Rick echoed.

"He didn't give his name," Marc said. "And I didn't recognize the voice."

"What did he want?"

"Your name. He wanted to know who was taking pictures at the crash scene this afternoon. So I told him."

Rick shrugged. "Sounds OK to me."

"I also told him he could find you at the Gazette," Marc went on. "OK?"

"Sure," Rick said. "I'm working here this week. So I'll be around." It was probably one of the search team who wanted a souvenir of the event.

"He said he'd call you in the morning." Then Marc continued, "Listen, I'm sorry about today."

"You're sorry?"

"I didn't—" he began and then stopped as though he was reconsidering what he had started to say. "You never got the flight you paid for."

"That wasn't your fault."

"I know. But. . . ." Marc's voice ran down. "Maybe we can do it tomorrow."

"Sure," Rick agreed. In the excitement of finding the wrecked plane, he had forgotten about the assignment that had put him in the helicopter in the first place. Starr News would still be waiting for those pictures. So would that newsmagazine in New York. "Tomorrow would be fine. Or even Wednesday."

"Better make it tomorrow," Marc said quickly. Almost too quickly, Rick thought. Why was it so important to go tomorrow? Marc offered no explanation, so Rick let it slide. Maybe the helicopter pilot had other plans—another flight assignment, perhaps.

"Are you OK?" Rick asked.

"Yeah," Marc said. "I'm fine."

Rick frowned at the phone for several long moments after he hung up. He had a strong, distinct feeling that there had been something more on Marc's mind when he called. Something he had intended to say, but which, for some reason, he couldn't bring himself to voice. Or was he letting his tired mind and overactive imagination take over again?

A sudden urge to yawn shattered the thought before it could go any further. What he needed most right then was a good eight or ten hours of sleep.

He reached for the strip of film. It was dry. All thirty-six of the tiny images looked good. He'd get those prints made and leave a selection—maybe six of the best shots—on the editor's desk upstairs. On the way home he'd drop a packet off with the courier service. Starr News would get them in San Francisco later that night. That would give them time to hit the morning papers that might be interested.

Rick muffled another long yawn and slipped a negative into the enlarger. He hadn't realized until just then how tired he really was. By the time he finished the job and started for home, the yawns were coming closer together.

Bed sounded like an excellent idea.

But tired as he was, sleep wasn't going to be allowed to come that easily. The shrilling of the telephone next to his bed took care of that. It seemed to happen not more than a few seconds after he'd crawled between the sheets and closed his eyes.

He fumbled for the receiver and snatched it up before a second ring could disturb the rest of the family.

"Rick?" It was his uncle, Brett Shannon, the owner and editor of the Gazette. "We've got a problem."

"Yeah?" Rick's tongue felt thick as he mumbled his answer. "What kind of a problem?"

"Burglary."

That one word was enough. Rick switched on his bedside lamp and squinted into the bright light.

"Someone broke into the Gazette tonight."

Suddenly the thought of sleep was gone. "The Gazette?" he echoed. "Did they get much?"

"I don't know," Brett Shannon said. "That's why I called you. It seems that the darkroom was the target."

T H R E E
NOTHING MISSING

Rick wasn't exactly sure what he expected to find
in the newspaper darkroom. A mess, probably.
Boxes and papers scattered all over the floor.
Some things broken. Drawers and cupboards
open. Confusion. That's the way they always
showed it on those TV detective programs.

It certainly wasn't what he found.

"Well?"

Rick turned at the sound of the voice. His uncle,
Brett Shannon, was standing in the door. Beside
him was a uniformed police officer.

"Rick. You know Sergeant Randall." Brett Shannon didn't believe in wasting time with small talk
or unnecessary questions.

Rick nodded. The White Valley police officer
was a regular visitor to the newspaper office.

"What happened?" Rick wanted to know.
"What's missing?"

"That's what we'd like you to tell us," Randall
said.

Rick's first reaction was to give them a quick
answer. Nothing was missing. As far as he could
see, nothing was even out of place. But instead he
turned and let his eyes run around the well
equipped darkroom one more time, noting all the
familiar items and cataloguing them quickly in his
mind. The three enlargers standing in their normal places on the bench along one wall. The big
sink and drainboard and the trays for holding the

photographic chemicals and solutions. The rack
that held the enlarged prints as they dried—five
of them stood there now, exactly as he had left
them. Two spare cameras on the shelf to the left.
Below them, boxes of enlarging paper and chemicals. Then there was the special lighting equipment, including six different-sized flash units,
plus a collection of heavy-duty extension cords.
Along the wall to the left of the door were three
filing cabinets, each with four drawers. Those
held the negatives and extra prints that were
stored for future reference and use.

In his quick survey of the darkroom Rick had
turned in a complete circle until he found himself
once again facing his uncle and Sergeant Randall.

"Well?" It was just a one-word question from
Brett Shannon. But coming from him, it was more
like a command for an immediate complete
report.

Rick shook his head. "Everything looks normal."

"You're sure?" Randall wanted to know.

"As sure as I can be," Rick answered. "The
equipment is all there. It looks just like I left it."

The police officer made his own quick visual
scan of the room. "OK," he said. "That checks with
the rest of the building. So I guess you were lucky
this time. Your janitor must have scared the guy
off before he had a chance to take anything." He
pointed to the shelf to the left of the enlargers.
"Those cameras, for example. Valuable but pretty
simple merchandise for a thief to unload. They'd
make a tempting and easy target."

Rick nodded his agreement. A camera wouldn't
be difficult to sell. "Tony saw him?"

Tony Martin, the night janitor for the Gazette, normally began his work between eleven and midnight when there wasn't much activity around the newspaper office to disturb his cleaning routine.

"Well," Randall said. "Not exactly."

Tony, who had walked up to the group at that moment, completed the reply. "Sorry Rick. I only saw his back as he ran down the hall." He shrugged apologetically. "I was a little late getting in tonight. There was another job I had to finish up first, so it must have been about ten past twelve when I opened the door to the big room upstairs. That's when I heard a noise down here. I figured it might be you working late on something, so I came to the top of the stairs and called your name, just to let you know I was here. Next thing I know this guy comes tearing out of the darkroom, down the hall, up the back stairs, and out that door into the alley." He paused and looked around at the three faces. "Did he take much?"

"Not a thing," the editor said. "Thanks to you."

Tony's face showed his surprise. "What'd I do?"

"He heard your voice in the middle of the night in a deserted building," Rick told him. "That was enough. You spooked him."

Sergeant Randall looked thoughtful as he put his notebook away. "I guess that about wraps it up. We'll put this one in the book as an amateur job—a spur-of-the-moment thing."

"Why do you say that?"

"You put your finger on it, Rick," the police officer told him as they walked toward the front door. "Panic. The guy spooked too easily. One word from Tony and he ran. Empty-handed. An experienced thief would at least have taken something for his efforts. He certainly wouldn't have left those cameras on the shelf. He was in the room. He had the opportunity. But he didn't touch them."

Rick nodded his agreement. What the police officer said sounded logical.

When they stepped out onto the sidewalk, the night air was still laced with bright pulses of blue and red light from the two police cars parked at the curb.

"Get a good night's sleep," Randall said as he stepped into the lead car. "There's nothing to worry about here. This guy won't be back. You can count on it." With a friendly salute, he was gone.

Sure, Rick muttered to himself. We'll get a good night's sleep for what little time is left—if the phone doesn't ring again. The black numbers on his digital watch said it was exactly 2:07 a.m.

The phone didn't ring. And the night wasn't quite as short as Rick feared.

As a matter of fact, he overslept.

It was after nine-thirty when he raced into the newspaper office on his way to the airport. He'd managed to grab a piece of toast and a half cup of coffee while he called Marc from the house to confirm that he was on his way for another flight.

Brett Shannon's voice met him two steps inside the front door. His uncle wasn't far behind the sound.

"What's this?" The editor waved a sheet of

yellow copy paper at him. "Nothing more than a name on that pilot?"

"That's it."

"No address? No relatives? How about where he worked?"

Rick shook his head.

"What time was the crash?"

"No one knows," Rick said. "There are a lot of things about that crash that have question marks hanging on them."

"Then find out!" Brett Shannon growled. "This is supposed to be a newspaper. That means we deal in facts. It also means we are expected to print the news while it is news, not after it's history." He jabbed at the paper with his index finger. "That was a local plane, so that means we're interested. Possibly—and very likely—the missing pilot was also local. In that case we have an even greater interest. Besides, I smell something more in this than a simple crash."

Rick took a step back.

But Brett Shannon wasn't finished. "It may not be as big a story as—," he pushed some papers around on his desk, picked up one, stared at it for a moment with a frown, and then dropped it again, "—laser weapons testing in the Mojave Desert." He looked up. "But there's something more there."

"Right, boss." Rick gave a salute and grinned. Even his uncle's Sunday school class of teenagers got that same growl from time to time, and loved every decibel of it.

The editor was still tossing words after him. "A telephone book can print names. As a newspaper, our readers have come to expect a few extra details—little things like who, where, when, what, and why."

Rick backed away and saluted again. "Aye, aye, sir. I'll see what I can find out."

"On the other hand, the pictures aren't bad." Coming from Brett Shannon, that was a blue ribbon compliment.

Rick was still grinning as he dived into the darkroom to grab some extra film, and the five prints he had promised to give to Marc. Halfway across the room he stopped and sniffed the air. It was strange, he thought, how a person could get used to certain smells when he worked with them regularly. Until that moment he had never realized just how long the pungent aroma of developer and the acidic smell of fixer hung in the air after a developing and printing session.

He flipped a wall switch to the right of the door and listened as the ventilator fan hummed to life. That would take care of the smell—something he should have done last night before he left. Normally he would have, but as tired as he had been, he likely forgot.

One more quick glance around the room told him that nothing had changed since his last look.

It was close to ten-thirty when Rick reached the airport and left his old car in the parking lot. Right on time.

The sky was a clear blue with scarcely a cloud in sight. The wind indicator on the top of one of the hangars was drooping. That meant there was no wind. For Rick, that was good news. It looked like a fine day for a flight. A fine day for picture taking, too. Calm, clear weather would certainly make the project a lot simpler, and much more pleasant. There was nothing like a vibrating, bucking helicopter to throw a picture out of focus.

Rick frowned slightly at the thought of photographing a small flood-control dam. Well, one day, maybe he'd get a chance for some interesting assignments.

As he swung his camera bag over his shoulder and pushed open the gate that led onto the field between the two big Blair hangars, he could hear the whining sound of a helicopter motor as the rotors began to turn. Probably Marc, getting ready for the flight, he guessed. That was one thing he'd noted yesterday—how carefully the pilot went over every item on his preflight checklist before they lifted off. He took nothing for granted.

Rick began to hurry. But before he could cover the length of the long hangar building the motor sound picked up in speed. An instant later a blue and white and orange bird swept into view as it climbed away to the east.

Marc was standing on the field staring after the departing helicopter when Rick rounded the corner. Even from that distance it was obvious that the young pilot was upset. It showed very clearly in the set of his shoulders and the angle of his jaw.

Rick stopped, uncertain. He had a feeling that he'd just missed the tail end of a good argument.

It was a full minute before Marc turned and noticed him.

"How long have you been standing there?" he demanded.

"Not long."

Marc looked doubtful.

"I just got here," Rick said.

Marc shot another glance at the helicopter. "Did you hear what that—what he said?" There was a bite to his voice.

Rick shook his head. "Who?"

"That—" he stopped, and cocked his head to one side, thinking. "You didn't hear, did you?"

"No."

"Maybe it's better that way," Marc said. He bit the words off.

Rick said nothing. It wasn't hard to see that the pilot's anger was close to the surface and that he was having a hard time keeping it down.

That mood lasted all the way out to the construction site for the new dam, and back again. Once or twice during the forty-five minute flight, Rick thought he caught what sounded like a muttered, "Pious hypocrite. . . ," but he couldn't be certain. It was difficult to hear clearly over the motor noise. Especially when Marc kept his intercom mike switched off for a good part of the flight.

Yesterday during the search for the missing plane, there had been worry in Marc's voice. Later Rick was sure he had noticed an unexplainable tone of fear. But today it was all anger.

The White Valley airport was in sight again on the return trip when Marc suddenly blurted his first comment that was longer than one syllable.

"Did you ever meet one of those religious guys who says he goes to church every Sunday?" There was a bite of bitterness in his voice.

Rick swallowed hard before answering. It wasn't exactly the kind of question he had expected. "Sure," he said. "Why?"

"Because that's what he says he does."

"Who?"

"That cousin of mine."

"The one who owns the planes?"

"The same. The one and only, Sam Blair."

"You mean he's a Christian?"

"I suppose so. He goes to church."

The anger was bubbling up again. Rick could feel it coming. Given the right spark to touch it off, that anger could erupt into the open like a volcano. But anger at what?

Why was Marc really angry? Because his cousin went to church? Or was he angry at everyone who went to church and called himself a Christian? If that was the case, Rick thought, his own friendly relationship with the young pilot would soon be coming to a screeching halt. Being a Christian was something that was an important part of his own life. Attending church was something that was on his regular schedule.

But then, maybe it was something else that ignited the anger spark in Marc—a family argument, a disagreement about work—and church was only an excuse for something or someone to blame.

"Was that your cousin who took off in the other helicopter when I arrived this morning?"

Marc nodded. "Yeah." He turned the Jet Ranger in a wide circle around the field. Then he lifted one hand briefly and pointed. "There he is now."

Rick leaned forward slightly for a better view. A solitary figure stood on the pavement in front of the Blair hangars. Even from several hundred feet up it wasn't difficult to see that Sam Blair's hands were planted firmly on his hips, his legs spread apart, his head tipped back.

"Your cousin?"

"That's him," Marc said. "You can tell by the way he holds the pavement down. It's only on Sunday that his feet don't touch the ground so hard. That's when he tucks his big black Bible under his arm and floats off to church. Twice. He sings hymns and smiles and puts his money in the plate and shakes hands with the preacher and shows everyone what a fine upstanding citizen he is. I saw him there one time." He snorted. "I see him the rest of the week, too, when he's here. That's when he takes off his church mask and the real Sam Blair stands up. And, boy does he stand up."

Rick's mind raced. There had to be something he could say that would cool the angry fire that was roaring in Marc's thoughts.

"Maybe they're all like that," the pilot went on. "Maybe they're all putting on a big act about how nice they are. Maybe all those people who sit in pews on Sunday morning put on special faces when they go to church. Like it's part of their uniform or something."

There was an answer for Marc. Rick knew it as

well as he knew his own name. But how could he say it in a way that wouldn't stretch Marc's anger even farther? A hundred times, it seemed, he'd watched his father or Brett Shannon answer questions and objections like Marc's. When no one was around Rick had even practiced those answers himself, like an actor preparing for a play. It worked fine then. He'd even recorded it on his cassette machine. When he listened to the playback it hadn't sounded like a bad effort. But then a real life situation like this came along and all those "good answers" and "well thought-out phrases" vanished in a jumble of one-syllable fumbles.

"No," Rick said at last. He was running out of time. "It's not that way. I can guarantee it."

"Yeah?" Marc's concentration on his flying didn't waver. His left hand twisted gently and just as gently he pushed forward on the control it was gripping. The helicopter began to lose altitude, dropping toward the yellow target on the pavement—its normal landing spot.

"You might be right," he went on. "I guess I wouldn't know much about that. I've never run into many of them. Except for that one down there."

The helicopter touched down smoothly on the pad in front of the hangar and the brief conversation was over. Marc switched off the ignition and leaned back in his seat.

"Now we get the news," he said. A grim sort of smile flickered across his lips. At that instant he seemed strangely relaxed. "Here comes our self-righteous judge and jury to tell us that Marc Blair has to go find himself a new job."

It took a second or two for the words to register in Rick's mind. "What do you mean?" he demanded.

Marc shrugged. "It's just a guess." He pushed his door open and jumped to the ground.

"Why—?"

Rick had no chance to finish the question. Sam Blair had started toward them the moment the helicopter's landing gear touched the pavement. He walked with a quick and determined stride.

"Marc!" He didn't even wait for the swishing whine of the rotors to die away before he began barking out his orders. He had a voice that would drill through any sound that might come in its way. "Shut her down and pack your gear. It's your last flight."

For a long moment Rick felt like he was glued to his seat. Marc stood rigid beside the helicopter, one hand resting against the curved plexiglass window. Rick could almost see the whirlpool of thoughts tearing around in the pilot's mind. Any moment he expected to hear an angry outburst. But it never came.

Overhead, the big blades gave their last swish, and a sigh, and became still.

Marc took a deep, slow breath. His shoulders slumped. When he turned and looked back at Rick, all trace of the anger had drained away. He slowly nodded his head.

"What did I tell you?" he said, then lowered his eyes.

F O U R
ACCUSATIONS

The roaring whine of a small executive jet warming up next to a nearby hangar filled the air and their ears with a noise that masked out every other sound.

Every sound that is, except one—the voice of Sam Blair.

"Did you hear what I said?" he demanded.

Marc stepped away from the helicopter. "I heard," he said. "I'm fired?"

"It might come to that when they finish the investigation. Until then you don't work around here."

Diplomacy might not be one of Sam Blair's strong points, Rick thought. But he did have to admit that the owner of Blair Aviation had a talent for getting right to the point when he had something on his mind.

Rick shot a glance toward the aircraft that was making all the noise, and noted the simple blue insignia on its tail. Now *there* was a company, whoever it was, that believed in traveling in style.

Sam Blair pivoted abruptly as Rick stepped around the front of the helicopter.

"Who are you?"

"Rick Shannon. White Valley Gazette and Starr News."

A strange mixture of emotions left their tracks across Sam Blair's face during the next five seconds. But he recovered quickly.

"You're that reporter that was along for the ride when they found the wreck of my plane?" Not quite a sneer, but close.

"Photographer mostly," Rick corrected, his voice as pleasant as he could make it. "Once in awhile a reporter. And you're right. I was there. As a matter of fact, Marc and I were the first on the scene. We were the ones who actually found your plane."

Sam Blair waved off that morsel of information as unimportant.

Rick opened a compartment in the top of his camera bag and took out the brown envelope he had put there earlier. He held it out. "Almost forgot. I thought you might like to have some copies so I brought these along."

"Copies of what?"

"Pictures," Rick said easily. "Photographs of the crash scene yesterday."

Sam Blair took the envelope and turned it over in his hand, but didn't open it. His eyes jumped from Rick to Marc and then back again. "I've already seen it," he snapped. "I don't need any pictures to tell me what my plane looks like."

Rick ignored the curt remark and exclaimed, "Of course. The crash investigation team. You were up there with them this morning. Any news?"

"Why do you think he's off the job?" Sam Blair's head jerked in Marc's direction.

"I was wondering about that."

"Incompetence."

Rick's lower jaw dropped.

"That plane didn't just crash," Sam Blair snapped. "The weather was good on the weekend, so we can't blame that. And it wasn't something simple like pilot error. The controls were locked. They'd been tampered with. The automatic pilot was damaged, or faulty."

"But," Rick protested, "what does that have to do with Marc?"

Sam Blair snorted. "Ask him," he said. "Just ask him who was the last one to handle the Cessna before it was rented out. Ask him who serviced it. Ask him who checked it over very thoroughly, and carefully—," his lips curled over the words as he emphasized them, "—and certified that it was ready for flight. Ask him who signed the service book for the plane that crashed forty minutes from here."

Rick looked questioningly at Marc, but the helicopter pilot didn't say a word.

"The way I see it," Sam Blair went on, "we're left with a choice between incompetence and sabotage."

Rick stared. He could scarcely believe what he was hearing.

"Sabotage?" he echoed.

"It's a possibility."

"Those are pretty serious words."

"That crash was serious, too, in case you've forgotten. A total wipeout. Even a small plane like that Cessna 172 costs money."

Rick nodded, straining to keep his emotions on an even keel. He was beginning to understand the anger Marc had shown earlier. Sam Blair didn't make it easy. Rick was tempted to ask about the insurance coverage on the wrecked plane, but the timing somehow didn't seem quite right. He took a deep breath. "How about the pilot? Any news yet of him?"

"No. None."

Perhaps it was just the emotion of the moment, Rick thought. Perhaps that's why the owner of the plane seemed to be showing so much more concern for the aircraft than for the pilot.

Sam Blair's eyes narrowed as he looked across the runway toward the distant mountains. "If it's not sabotage, then it's downright careless incompetence. How else do you explain why an otherwise healthy piece of equipment suddenly develops fatal faults—a piece of equipment that was certifed OK by the person who checked out that aircraft less than two hours before it took off?"

"Any number of things could have happened."

"Not in my books."

For some reason, Sam Blair had already made up his mind, and he wasn't about to let any other possibilities interfere.

Again Rick looked at the helicopter pilot, and wondered. Why didn't he say something? Why didn't he at least make some kind of protest? Only a few minutes before they landed Marc had had plenty to say about his cousin. But now he just stood there, strangely silent, taking it all.

"Aren't you jumping to conclusions?" Rick tried again. "The investigation team hasn't filed any reports yet."

"That's why he isn't officially fired—yet. Not until the investigation is completed." Sam Blair left no doubt as to what he expected from that report. With that he whirled around and stalked away back to his office, effectively cutting off any further conversation or questions. The loud slam of the office door added the final forceful punctuation.

Rick suddenly discovered that sometime in the last few seconds he had taken a deep breath and that he was still holding it. Now he let it slide out in a long, low-pitched whistle. For a time he could only gaze at the closed door and slowly shake his head.

"Well," Marc said at last, with a heavy sigh. "Now you've met him. In person."

"Is he always like that?"

"Sometimes less. Sometimes more. Especially the last few months."

"And before that?"

Marc shrugged. "I don't know. I've only worked for Sam for about a year."

There was no anger there now, Rick noted. Not even bitterness. "Limp and lifeless" was the description that came to his mind. Marc's voice reminded him of a balloon with all the air gone.

"He didn't mean—" Rick began.

Marc held up a hand. "Sure he did. All of it." He looked down at his feet. "Part of what Sam said was true. I'll give him credit for that much."

Rick looked his question.

"He was right. I did service that plane," Marc explained. "I checked it over, and I signed for it.

The mechanic who normally works on Saturday morning was sick, so I filled in for him for a couple of hours. I refueled the Cessna. I locked the doors. And I left it where we always park the rental planes."

"And everything was OK?"

"Perfect. The checklist is in the book."

"What about the automatic pilot your cousin mentioned?"

"The mechanic took the plane up on Friday for a thorough test flight. It's a regular safety routine around here. Eveything was working normally then. There were no problems with the controls at that time, or when I checked it out. What happened up in the mountains, I don't know."

Rick bent down to fasten the straps on his camera bag. He fumbled with them a little longer than necessary to give his hands something to do.

"You knew your cousin was going to blame you?"

Marc nodded.

"Why?"

"It doesn't matter."

Rick straightened and studied his companion. Marc remained silent.

On their flight back from the construction site Marc had been full of opinions as to what motivated Sam Blair. He'd known exactly what his cousin was going to say when they landed. Now suddenly it wasn't important to him? Why? What had changed?

Maybe it was none of his business, Rick thought. Maybe it wasn't as serious as it sounded. Maybe he really had stumbled into the middle of a family argument—a personality clash. That kind of thing could occasionally happen in the best of families. Once in awhile those arguments could get pretty warm, and then words might be used that were stronger than necessary or intended.

Of course, there was always the possibility, he supposed, that there was a grain of truth in what Sam Blair had said. After all, Marc was human. That meant he could make mistakes. He could be careless.

Was that why the pilot didn't protest? Was there something he wasn't telling? Was there something he had overlooked when he serviced the plane—something he hadn't corrected?

Rick shook off that idea. It was possible, he supposed. Anything was. And it was true that he didn't know Marc Blair very well. But somehow, after being in the air with him for ten or twelve hours yesterday, and another couple of hours that morning, he couldn't imagine him being careless about anything connected with flying. It just didn't fit.

While Rick watched, Marc locked the door of the helicopter. He patted the blue and orange machine a couple of times, glanced up at the big blades of the rotor, then let his eyes run along the smooth lines of the Bell Jet Ranger back to its unique tail assembly. He slowly walked around the helicopter, inspecting it and wiping off small streaks of oil and grime, until he was standing next to Rick.

"She's a good bird," Marc murmured.

It would take a blind man not to see that flying meant a great deal to him. He patted the helicopter one more time, like a cowboy saying a final good-bye to a favorite horse, then turned away.

"I'm sorry you had to get mixed up in that," Marc said softly.

Rick groped for words, but the ones that said what he wanted to say were out of reach.

"Could you give me a ride into town?" Marc's voice cut in.

"Sure," Rick said. He glanced toward the office, a puzzled look on his face. "You're leaving? Just like that?"

Marc shrugged. "Why not? There's nothing more I can do here. Sam meant what he said. It's his company. If he wants to fire me, that's his privilege."

"I suppose so," Rick agreed slowly. "And of course you know him better than I do. But—," he broke off momentarily. "It's just that . . . well. . . ."

"You think I'm giving up because maybe what Sam said was right."

"I didn't say that," Rick protested.

"No, you didn't," Marc said. "But the thought has crossed your mind. Hasn't it?"

"I. . . ." Rick's voice trailed off. It was true. He had thought about it.

Marc scuffed at a clump of grass with his foot. "Maybe I did do something wrong," he said. "Not on purpose. That I can guarantee. But maybe I was careless for a moment and overlooked something important. I don't know. I can't really be sure." Troubled eyes met Rick's. "But, one thing I do know. Arguing with Sam Blair isn't going to change his mind about anything."

They had been walking slowly toward the gravel parking lot. Now as they reached the car, Rick opened the door and swung his camera case onto the rear seat.

"What now?" Rick asked, but his question was drowned out by a blast of noise. The jet that had been warming up earlier chose that precise moment to begin its takeoff. "What will you do now?" Rick repeated, turning to follow the smooth climbing of the little jet.

Marc shrugged again, and sighed. "Maybe *they* need a helicopter pilot."

"Who?"

"Preston." Marc's right hand raised briefly to point in the direction of the departing plane.

"Preston?" Rick echoed. "Preston Laser-Optics?"

"You know the outfit?"

Rick nodded. "Sort of. We just about flew over their place this morning. They've got a research center north of here about ten or fifteen miles. Another place down near the Mojave Desert where they do special testing. Something else over in Nevada."

"Big stuff, huh?"

"Yeah." Rick thought of the laser weapons testing Brett Shannon had mentioned that morning. Preston was big enough and important enough to be doing stuff like that. "You might be able to get a job with them," he said. "If you can get the security clearance."

"Tough?"

"That's what I hear. They do a lot of top secret work for the government."

Marc made a face. "It was an idea." He looked

back up at the plane, which now was no more than a dark speck against the white of a cloud. "A stupid idea at that. There's not much chance I could get any kind of flying job around here until after the investigation. Not while I'm suspended from this one. Word gets around."

Rick nodded his sympathy. Marc was probably right. It would be tough to do anything with that hanging over his reputation. News like that had a way of traveling fast.

He shook his head silently as he slipped into the driver's seat. The week had certainly picked a fantastic way to start. A plane crash with a missing pilot. A break-in with nothing taken. Marc fired from his job, supposedly because of the plane crash. And this was only Tuesday afternoon. With that kind of a beginning, he could imagine what the rest of the week was going to be like.

Several times on the road into town he looked over at Marc, started to speak, then changed his mind. The pilot was slumped low in the passenger seat, silently gazing out the window.

He hadn't budged an inch by the time Rick parked next to the Gazette building. Even a fire engine screaming past hadn't roused him.

"Can I drop you off someplace?" Rick asked.

Marc stirred, glanced at his watch, and then shook his head. "It's OK. I can walk." But he didn't move.

Rick let several long silent seconds slip by, then asked, "You want to come in for a minute?" After what had happened, it might be good for the pilot to have some company and a change of scenery and activity. At least it might help him to get his mind off his troubles for a few minutes.

There was no immediate reaction. Then Marc blinked, and looked up at the WHITE VALLEY GAZETTE sign over the door. For the first time he seemed to notice where they were. He sat up. "Sure," he said, the beginnings of a smile lighting the corners of his eyes. "I think I'd like that."

"Great." Rick forced an extra helping of cheerfulness into his voice. "I'll give you the grand tour." He reached into the back seat for his camera bag. "It shouldn't take me more than a couple of minutes to package these films. Then we can run over to Ernie's and grab a hamburger or something." The café around the corner from the Gazette building was a regular stop for the newspaper staff.

But before the tour could start, Brett Shannon's voice stopped them cold, a half dozen steps into the front hall.

"Shannon!"

Marc looked startled.

Rick grinned. "I should have warned you about that."

Before he could say anything more, Brett Shannon was in the hall with them. There was no twinkle in his eye this time. "He came back."

"Who?"

"Our sneak thief from last night."

Rick's eyes widened. "He tried again? In broad daylight?"

"No," the editor said. "We only just discovered it an hour ago. But he was here sometime before eight this morning—before the first person came in. There's a broken window in that little room down by the back door. We think that's how he got in this time."

Rick stared. Two break-ins in one night? It wasn't possible.

MISSING PICTURES?

Rick's mind spun as he and Marc followed the editor into the newsroom.

A second break-in!

"Then the police were wrong," Rick exclaimed. "It was a planned effort after all. Tony did scare him off the first time. But when things quieted down he came back to finish the job. No one would expect. . . ." His voice trailed off as he noticed that his uncle was shaking his head.

"You're a photographer," Brett Shannon said. "Use your eyes."

Rick did. And what he saw told him that the Gazette's editorial office looked about the same as it always did. There was no more clutter than usual on the desks. Typewriters, telephones, computer terminals, the radio for monitoring police and emergency frequencies, and the tape recorders. And of course there were the reporters and writers pounding their keyboards.

"What do you see?"

"The normal things."

"Exactly."

Rick stared at his uncle briefly and then let his eyes circle the room one more time. "He didn't—"

"I'm glad to see that your mind has decided to keep you company," Brett Shannon growled. He pulled a chair out from behind his desk and dropped into it. "Your brilliant photographic powers of observation have finally noticed the obvious." He nodded solemnly, but with a sparkle in his eye. "That's good. We might make a reporter out of you yet."

The editor's arm swept in a wide circle that took in the entire editorial office. "Of course with the kind of confusion that is normal around this place, who can tell for sure if something is missing. We once lost a reporter in here. Found him three days later under a pile of papers on his desk. Of course, I wouldn't mention any names."

A half dozen heads popped up around the room and grinned. Brett Shannon's good-natured growling was legendary.

It made no sense, Rick thought. Why would anyone risk breaking into a newspaper office—twice in one night—but not take anything? Once was understandable. But twice? Was their mysterious visitor stupid? Or desperate?

The editor swung around to his keyboard as though, suddenly, the boys didn't exist. Rick took the hint and backed away. "I'll take another look downstairs."

"You do that," Brett Shannon said. His fingers were already pounding the keys as he spoke. "And tell your friend there—the one you didn't bother to introduce—that helicopter pilots are always welcome."

"I—"

"Now get out of here. We're running a newspaper. Not a monthly magazine."

"Aye, aye, sir." Rick grinned as he headed for the door.

"How does he know who I am?" Marc wanted to know a moment later as they hurried down the stairs.

Rick laughed. "You've heard the story about elephants and their memories? Well, they're strictly amateurs when matched against him."

"But I never even met him before today," Marc protested.

"Doesn't matter," Rick said. He led the way into the darkroom. "Likely he saw you once when he was out at the airport on business."

"And he remembered?"

"Not only you. He knows half the people in town by name."

"That's hard to believe."

"I guess it is," Rick admitted. "But he does have a phenomenal memory. I've known him just about all my life, so I should be used to it by now, but every once in awhile he surprises me, too." He grinned at Marc's puzzled expression. "Sometimes he's my boss. The rest of the time he's my uncle."

Marc's eyes narrowed. "A boss and a relative with a memory like that could be a problem. He could be hard to work for. He'd remember every mistake you ever made."

"Not him."

"But. . . ." Marc looked very doubtful. "He—"

"All that shouting and growling," Rick said. "Is that what's bothering you? Doesn't mean a thing." After the little demonstration by Sam Blair out at the airport, he could understand why Marc had his doubts. "It's all part of his act. Actually he's really great. Underneath all that noise he's soft as a marshmallow. That's why he does it, I guess. Doesn't want anyone to know what a soft-touch he really is." Was that a hurt expression that flashed across Marc's face for an instant? "That's my theory, anyhow."

Marc shook his head. "If you say so."

Rick grinned as he opened his camera bag and took out the three films he had shot that morning. "I haven't met anybody yet who doesn't like the guy. That includes some local politicians who have found themselves on the wrong end of one of his editorials." He popped the films into a special padded envelope that was already addressed to Starr News.

"Why?"

Rick leaned back against the counter. "For one thing, I guess, there's nothing phony about the guy. What you see is what you get."

Marc snorted. "If that's true he must have a different brand of religion than Sam."

Rick looked up, startled.

"I saw that motto on your uncle's desk," Marc said.

Rick nodded. He'd forgotten about the little sign reading God Cares—Do You? Brett Shannon had slid it under the glass top of his desk. Well, at least it opened up the possibility of conversation on the subject. But what could he say? He couldn't just blurt out, "Brett Shannon's like that because he's a Christian." He could guess Marc's reaction to that. That brief expression of pain that had flashed across the young pilot's face a moment ago had carried a thousand words with it.

"Yeah," Rick agreed at last. "I think you might be right. The difference is that for Brett Shannon, God is part of his life every day."

Marc started to react with a sharp retort. But before any sound came he snapped his mouth closed again, turned and took three strides across the room. He stopped and toyed with one of the enlargers briefly, then murmured, "I guess you're right." And before Rick could say anything further, he swung around. "You about done here?"

Rick took a breath. "Just about."

He scribbled a hurried note to the darkroom technician at Starr News and added it to the envelope. To save time, these films would be processed in their lab.

"What was all the talk up there about a break-in?" Marc wanted to know. The momentary flash of annoyance was gone.

"Just what you heard," Rick said. He quickly brought him up to date.

Marc looked around the little room. "Maybe he wanted one of your pictures."

Rick laughed. "I have to admit, in all modesty, I'm a pretty good photographer. But not *that* good. The kind of shots I take will never make it into any art gallery. They're news pictures. Not collector's items." As he spoke, he sealed the envelope and dropped it onto the counter.

"Maybe so," Marc said. "But this guy tried twice. He was persistent. So there must have been something here he wanted—something valuable. You say he didn't take any equipment. So what else is there?"

"That's what I keep asking myself," Rick said.

As he spoke, a thought—a small memory—flickered at the edge of his mind. It was there for just an instant. Something he should remember. But then it was gone again.

"Whoever he was," he went on, "he knew his way around a darkroom. If he moved anything for any reason, then he also happened to be observant enough to put things back exactly as he found them."

"What are you saying?" Marc questioned. "That he broke in here to use the equipment?"

Rick frowned. Now there was an idea. Would someone do that? "It's possible," he said slowly. "But why would he go to so much trouble? There's a place in town where you can rent a complete darkroom for one hour, two hours, five hours—whatever time you need. The equipment is good—as good as anything we have in here."

"OK," Marc said with a shrug. "What other reason would there be? As they say in all the detective books, there has to be a motive."

"Sure," Rick agreed. "There probably is. But we'll probably never know what it was. I do know one thing: there aren't any pictures in here worth stealing. We also know he didn't take any cameras or film. And I certainly see no good reason why he should break in to use any of the equipment." He picked up the film package and started for the door. "So maybe we'll never know the answer. In the meantime, I don't know about you, but I sure have a compelling motive to attack a triple-size hamburger."

Marc grinned his agreement.

But they weren't going to escape quite so easily.

The shrill sound of the telephone took care of that before Rick's fingers even touched the door handle. It was the pressroom. They had damaged a print. They needed a replacement. And as usual, the deadline was "immediately."

"Right now?" Rick repeated into the phone. His stomach growled on cue. Why couldn't someone, just once, want something tomorrow? Why did everything in the life of the newspaper have to be so urgent? "We were just leaving for lunch," he pointed out. "A very late lunch." The hint was ignored. "OK," he said with a resigned sigh. "Which one is it? . . . Number 11? . . . Same size? . . . Uh-huh . . . Ten minutes." He hung up the phone and tossed his film package onto the table by the door.

Marc backed into the room with an amused grin. "Does this kind of thing happen often?"

"Often enough," Rick said. Even on a small-town paper like the Gazette, life was one long string of deadlines.

"Anything I can do?"

"No, thanks." Rick reached for a red loose-leaf binder. "This'll only take a couple of minutes."

The loose-leaf file was arranged with two pages for each film. On the left-hand side was the proof sheet—the contact print of the strips of negatives arranged side by side so that one sheet of photographic paper held a tiny copy of each picture of an entire roll of 35mm film. Next to it in the binder was the transparent sheet holding the negatives—each strip of five pictures in its own slot.

"All I need now," he murmured, as much to

himself as to Marc, "is number 11 from the pictures I took yesterday at the crash scene." He flipped to the back of the book where he would find the most recent additions to the file. His hand froze in midair.

The proof sheet was missing.

But that couldn't be. Only once in awhile, when he was in a great hurry, had he forgotten to run off a proof sheet. But not this time. He was sure of it. It was the first thing he had done after developing and drying the film. He distinctly remembered printing up the proof sheet. And he remembered using it to select the negatives he would enlarge. He was almost certain, too, that he had put it in its proper place in the red binder.

And then he shrugged. Obviously he was wrong. It wasn't there. So, for once his memory wasn't as good as he thought it was. Not that it really mattered, he supposed. One missing proof sheet wasn't a disaster. It likely would show up eventually.

The problem wasn't serious—just slightly inconvenient. He removed the page of negatives from the book and held it up to the light. All he had to do was select the negative by its number. The pressroom had given him that from his note on the back of the damaged print.

Number 11 was what they wanted, so number 11 it would be. He squinted at the tiny black numerals printed along the bottom edge of the film. "There it is." He studied the tiny image a moment, then carefully pulled the strip of negatives from the protective sleeve.

For some reason that he couldn't explain, Rick ran his eyes over the rest of the negatives. As he reached the bottom of the page, his neck muscles stiffened. He stared a moment, and then pulled the transparent page closer for a better look.

The tiny black numerals along the edge of the film seemed to leap out at him.

Number 11!

"Something wrong?" Marc questioned.

"I don't know," Rick said. "I'm not sure." He picked up the strip of negatives that he had removed from the page and rechecked the tiny figures.

Number 11. Again.

But that couldn't be. They didn't make films with two sets of identical numbers on one roll.

"Different film," Marc suggested when Rick pointed out the problem.

"No," Rick replied. He scanned the pictures one more time. "I only shot one roll of film yesterday. I'm certain of that. Real certain." How could he forget the mental scolding he had given himself for not taking any spare film. "Thirty-six negatives. And that's how many are in this page."

"Then how could—"

"Wait a minute," Rick cut in. "There's something strange here." He leaned in for a closer examination, as his finger jabbed at one row of the negatives. "This strip is not from my camera."

"But you just said they were all there."

"They are."

"Then those five are extras that got mixed in by mistake."

"Nope," Rick said. "No extras. With a roll of thirty-six there's no room for extras in one of these file sheets. These are all mine. I recognize them."

Marc looked a little dazed. "I must have missed something in there somewhere," he said. "Those negatives are all of pictures that you took yesterday—on one roll of film. That's what you just said. So how could five of them not be from your camera?"

"That's what I'd like to know."

Marc looked blank.

"The duplicate numbers," Rick told him. "Normal 35mm films, like anyone can buy off the shelf, are numbered from one to twenty, or one to thirty-six."

Marc nodded. "That much I understand."

"The highest number here is 31. The last five numbers are missing, but no *pictures* are missing." Rick picked up the negative file sheet again. "There's one more little detail that most people aren't aware of, because for the most part it doesn't make any difference. It's something I discovered a while ago when I was working on some double-exposure special effects. For that I had to be sure the film was perfectly in position. Look." He held the negatives up to the light. "Notice how the sprocket holes along the edge line up with the pictures?"

"Right at the corner," Marc said after a moment's study.

"Correct," Rick said. "Now look at this strip of film—the one I said was taken with a different camera. Notice anything?"

Marc squinted at first one and then the other strip of film. "They don't match," he said at last. "They've moved over. Not much. Just a fraction of an inch. Maybe only a millimeter."

"That's right," Rick said. "Except that the holes didn't move. On a very old camera where the gears are half worn out, the winder might slip a bit every now and then or it might wind unevenly. But not on my camera. It's almost new, and it's definitely consistent. You can tell by looking at the rest of the film. There's an even space between each of the pictures."

Marc nodded his agreement.

"Every camera is unique," Rick went on. "With so many million of them around now, it is very likely that a lot of them do line up so closely it would be impossible to tell them apart. But not this time. There's a big enough difference to be noticeable."

"And that says this piece of film was taken with a different camera?"

"That's what it says to me." Rick pulled the offending strip of negatives from its slot in the transparent page. "And I think now we know what our sneak visitor was doing in here last night." He held the negatives up to the light. "He was making copies."

Then that little item at the edge of his memory suddenly came clear—that lingering smell of developer he had noticed in the room that morning. The aroma hadn't remained in the air as long as he thought. He had left the ventilator fan on when he left last night. But someone had turned it off. And their night visitor had neglected to leave it on when he was finished. That's why the chemical smells had still been noticeable.

Marc shook his head doubtfully. "So, if all this guy wanted was copies, why didn't he just take the negatives and then make himself some prints? Wouldn't that have been easier?"

"Sure it would," Rick said. "Much easier. And to make it even more simple he didn't have to break in here at all to get a copy of any of those pictures. He could walk through the front door up there any time during working hours and ask for one. We would have done it for him, no questions asked, for just a small charge. It would have been quite simple." He thoughtfully tapped a finger against the edge of the counter for a moment before adding, "But then, maybe he wanted something more than a copy."

"What else?"

"He took five of the original negatives and left us with five copies. Does that tell you anything?"

"He was in a hurry, and put the wrong strip back in the file," Marc suggested.

"It could be," Rick agreed. "But why did he make copies of the negatives. Most people just want prints." His eyes narrowed in a thoughtful squint. "Could it be that he wanted to keep the originals for himself." He paused to let the idea sink in.

"But why?"

Rick took a deep breath and let it trickle out slowly. "Because," he began, and hesitated. Was he reaching too far for an explanation? "Because maybe there was something in those original pictures he didn't want us to see."

SIX
ONE MISSING FACE

The red numerals on the darkroom's big digital clock counted off a full sixty seconds.

Marc picked up the negatives, examined them briefly, and then put them down again. "What are you trying to say? That he changed something in the pictures when he made the copies?"

Rick nodded. "It can be done. Take away some little detail. Or even add one."

Marc looked doubtful. "That would be pretty tricky."

"Sure it would," Rick agreed. "But it can be done."

Again Marc picked up the strip of negatives. "But these are all pictures of the plane crash," he protested.

"That's right."

"So, why would anyone want to change . . . anything. . . ?" Marc's voice ran down as the full implication sank in. For a second or two he was silent. "You think the plane crash wasn't an accident. You think there was something in those pictures that proved it. You—"

Rick shrugged. "When you add everything together, it does begin to look a little strange, doesn't it? A plane goes down in the mountains, but the pilot is missing. That same night this place is broken into and pictures of that crash are the only items touched. To me that's pretty strong evidence that there's a connection."

"But you don't know for sure that these pictures have been changed," Marc protested. "They could be exactly the same as the originals."

He was right, Rick thought. But why else would someone go to so much trouble if there wasn't something to hide?

He noted the frown on Marc's face as he gazed down at the sheet of negatives. The young pilot's left fist clenched and unclenched. Several times his mouth opened as though he was about to say something, but no sound came.

At last he looked up, his eyes troubled. "Do you think I—?"

"No," Rick interrupted with a shake of his head. "Not you." He was certain of that now. Sam Blair's loud outburst that afternoon, and the accusations he'd tossed around, had raised some doubts. But somehow there was something about Sam that made it difficult to put a great deal of confidence in what he said. The more he thought about Sam and Marc, the more he was sure that the helicopter pilot was in the clear. He had nothing to back up the feeling—at least nothing that would impress a police officer or a lawyer—but he was certain just the same.

"Who?"

It was Rick's turn to let a silent moment slide by. He hadn't had time yet to work out his idea. "I don't know," he said. "Maybe that phone call yesterday—"

"—asking who took the pictures of the wreck," Marc finished.

Rick nodded.

"I gave him the directions."

"You had no way of knowing."

"But—"

"That still doesn't tell us who it was," Rick cut in quickly. "Or why."

Marc cocked his head thoughtfully. "But if he—whoever it was—removed something from a picture, wouldn't it show?"

"Maybe," Rick said. "Maybe not." He opened a drawer and took out a small object that looked something like a fountain pen with a thin rubber pipe attached. "This is an airbrush," he said. "With a tool like this, a professional can make changes to a photograph that are almost impossible to spot. He can begin with a good sharp enlargement of the picture, do whatever he wants to the print, and then, if he wants, he can then rephotograph it onto another film."

"That's how they fix up tiny flaws in a picture?"

"Not only that," Rick said. "I've seen where a photographer completely removed one person from a group picture. Then the background was filled in to take his place. Without the original picture to compare it with, no one would ever notice the difference. I even read once where a foreign government used that technique to remove one certain man from every picture they had that included him. In their files, he wasn't there anymore. It was like he had never existed."

"And you think the guy who did this was that good with an airbrush?"

"I wouldn't be surprised."

"Why?"

"He left a few clues."

Marc looked around. "Like what?"

"Like the way he cleaned up after himself." Rick waved a hand in a motion that took in the darkroom. "If one of those chemical bottles was out of position, I'd know it. Everything has its special place. That way if I need something in the dark I don't have to hunt all over the room to find it. Every photographer has his own unique habits. Our friend knew that. He knew that if something was out of place, we'd notice. He knew precisely what he was doing with this equipment, and —," he leaned over the big wastepaper basket in the corner, "—he cleaned up after himself. He didn't leave any of his test prints for us to find. He covered his tracks pretty well."

"Except for the numbers," Marc said.

"That was his one little mistake," Rick agreed. "He forgot about the numbers. Or he was too pushed for time last night to get that little item right, and he hoped we wouldn't notice."

Several seconds ticked by. "Wouldn't it have been easier to take the negatives? Why make it so complicated?"

It was a good question. Why not just take the negatives? Unless—"We'd have discovered the missing pictures eventually. But this way, if the pressroom hadn't asked for one by number we might never have noticed that there was anything out of the ordinary. This way, at least, he was sure of giving himself a little extra time." Was that all he wanted? Time? Was he only playing for a little extra time?

And then what?

"The pictures won't tell us anything?" Marc's question cut in.

"They might," Rick said, "if we could compare them with the originals." He smiled faintly. "But there's another problem. There are five negatives in that strip. Was one of them changed? Or all of them?"

He glanced up at the clock and abruptly came to life again. Five minutes to three. He'd promised the pressroom a replacement for that damaged picture. If he didn't take care of it right away he'd be hearing some loud noises from that direction any second. Automatically he switched on the power to one of the big enlargers with one hand and reached for the negative carrier with the other.

"I'll print them up anyway," he said. "All five of the copies he left us. Plus that other picture I was supposed to have taken care of twenty minutes ago. Maybe one of us will notice something. Maybe he didn't do as perfect a job as I think he did."

But a half hour later the brief spurt of enthusiasm had faded. The replacement picture had been printed, developed, dried and delivered. Each of the five suspect negatives had likewise been enlarged, and processed. And each of them had been closely studied.

Marc rubbed his eyes as he backed away from the counter. "I don't even know what I'm looking for."

Rick wasn't sure that he did either. A flaw, perhaps. A cover-up job that was less than perfect. Evidence of a moment of carelessness in processing. But if any one of the pictures had been changed, it certainly didn't show. There wasn't a mark on the plane that didn't look like it belonged there.

"I don't see anything," Marc said. "The plane is a mess. Other than that, I don't see anything out of the ordinary. But I guess we're not supposed to, are we?"

Rick shook his head. "That's the general idea."

He picked up one of the prints, glanced at it, then dropped it onto the counter once again. Somewhere in all of this there was an answer, something they were missing. Something to tie the loose ends together. If they were right in their deductions so far, then someone had gone to a great deal of trouble to hide whatever might have been in one of those pictures.

Rick's eyes narrowed thoughtfully. "Maybe we should think about that. What are we looking for? What kind of evidence—of anything—would show on the outside of a plane after it crashed?"

"What do you mean?"

"I took some pictures of the cockpit and the inside of the plane," Rick said, speaking quickly in an effort to keep up with his thoughts. "But they're not in these five. These are all outside shots. A couple of them were even taken from a short distance away to give an idea of the general layout. So what could possibly be on the outside of a plane that anyone would want to hide?"

Marc looked thoughtful. "Nothing that I know of. Not on one of ours." He came back to the counter and ran his eyes across the prints. "Besides, there were seven of you there at the time. If there was anything that strange in plain sight, one of you would have noticed it."

"I don't know much about planes."

"Maybe not," Marc agreed. "But the other guys did. Everyone else who was in on the search had some experience with flying—mostly pilots and mechanics."

Rick thought back to the afternoon in the mountain valley. They had all closely examined the wrecked plane. He remembered particularly noticing how each of the men had wanted to see for himself. How they had each tried the door to be sure it wouldn't open.

"No one said anything."

"So," Marc said, waving his hand at the pictures. "If there was nothing there, then what have we been doing? This is a waste of time."

"No." Rick wasn't going to give up that easily. Someone had been using his darkroom and he wanted to know why. "Maybe we've been looking in the wrong place. We've concentrated on the plane itself. Perhaps something fell off or out of the plane and was lying on the ground some- where nearby."

"Sure," Marc said with a slight touch of sarcasm. "Or maybe one of the men on the search team was goofing off from work and he didn't want his picture in the paper because his boss might find out."

Rick started to laugh, but stopped midway. His mouth dropped open. He snapped his fingers. "Wait! You could be right. Not missing evidence. A missing *face.*"

"Now look," Marc protested. "I was just kidding. I—"

But Rick was already bending over the spread

of pictures once more, counting the figures standing around the plane. If someone was missing from the scene, it should be easy to tell.

Six.

They were all there then. His sudden feeling of anticipation faded.

"Whoever broke in here last night knew that pictures were being taken at the crash scene yesterday. Who could that have been, besides you?"

Marc shrugged. "Any of the guys on the search team, I suppose," he said slowly. "Any one of those who landed at the wreck sure would know. You weren't keeping it a secret."

"Six on the ground," Rick murmured. "Plus two helicopter pilots."

"And don't forget the rest of the aircraft. There were at least five more. Two men to each plane. They'd find out, too. The word would get around. One of the guys would be sure to mention there was a photographer on the scene."

The list of potential suspects was growing. "Do you know everyone who was out there yesterday?" Rick asked.

"No chance," Marc said. "Some of the guys were from White Valley. I might know them, or I could find out. But the rest of them. . . ." He shrugged. "A couple of planes came over from Sacramento. But the others, I don't know."

And even if they somehow managed to scrape up a list of the names of everyone who might have been involved with the search, Rick thought, it would take a good deal of time to check them all out.

"So we're right back where we started from," Marc murmured. "We don't know who did it, and we don't know what he did. We don't really even know why."

He was right, Rick thought. They had accomplished absolutely nothing except make a flimsy connection between the crash of a plane in the Sierras and a pair of break-ins in a newspaper office.

Absentmindedly he picked up one of the prints again, remembering the scene of the crash. Remembering the feeling of frustration. Remembering where he stood as he took the picture. Remembering the dejected look on the faces of those who had gone into the woods following the back-trail of the Cessna. Remembering. . . .

Six men had been landed by the search helicopters. Four had gone down the valley into the woods, and when they came back they had found nothing except a—

"Hey! We were right!" Rick blurted. "There *is* a missing face."

The sudden outburst caught Marc by surprise. He could only stare.

"The injured hiker," Rick continued. "He was in this picture. But he isn't there now. I remember exactly where he was standing." His finger jabbed at an empty spot near the edge of the trees. "Right there."

COVERED TRACKS

"The hiker?" Marc echoed.

Rick pushed the enlargement along the counter. "Right. He was in the picture. He had just come out of the woods and he was standing at the edge of the clearing." His finger indicated the spot. "When you know where to look, and what to look for, it's not so hard. See those two tree trunks? The markings aren't as sharp as on the others."

Marc studied the print briefly through a magnifying glass. "If you say so."

"I told you this guy would be good," Rick said. "Besides, we were looking for the wrong thing in the wrong place."

Marc shook his head doubtfully. "You're sure?"

"Positive." And he was. The scene, at the time he took the picture yesterday afternoon, was vividly clear in his mind.

"But, why. . . ?" Marc began. "Why would he want to hide his picture? It makes no sense. Last I heard, there was no law against hiking in the mountains."

No. Marc was right. There was nothing illegal about being there. Hundreds of people hiked those trails every year, especially the Pacific Crest trail that began somewhere down near the Mexican border and stretched along a meandering sort of route all the way to Canada. It was rugged country up there in the Sierra Nevadas, dotted with hundreds of great little lakes and streams.

Each of those who hit the trail up there had a different reason for doing it. Some just liked the view. Some went for the exercise. Some for the fishing or photography. Some went to get away from the tensions and pressures of their jobs. While others, perhaps, had more personal reasons for wanting to get away from civilization for awhile.

"Could he have been running from something?" Rick said. "Or someone? Maybe bill collectors. Or relatives."

"Or the police?"

Any one of them was possible. Some people wanted privacy more than others. But to want it bad enough to break in to a newspaper office— that was desperation.

"Does anyone know who that hiker was?" Rick wondered. "Did anyone get a name?"

"I don't know. I don't think so."

Rick's mind was flooded with questions. "Which helicopter brought him back? Did anyone talk to him on the way in? What happened after they landed? He was injured—a sprained ankle, or something. At any rate, he was limping. Did anyone give him a lift into town? To the hospital? Did—"

"Hold it." Marc's hand was up to halt the sudden stream of questions. He looked a little dazed. "I don't know any of the answers."

"Where can we find out?"

"You didn't see which chopper took him?"

"We left first," Rick pointed out.

Marc chewed his lip thoughtfully. "Rod might know," he said at last. "Rod Kemper. He was there, and he owns a sports shop over on Central."

"I know the place," Rick said. "That's only two blocks." He picked up his film package again and started for the door. "We'll drop this off on the way." The courier company office was on the same street.

After a quick five-minute walk in the fresh air, Rick felt the blood beginning to flow in his brain again.

Kemper's Sporting Goods had been in White Valley for as long as he could remember. Like most stores of its kind, it carried a full selection of fishing gear, hunting rifles, sports equipment for most of the team sports like football and base-ball, plus hiking gear. And for those who were of a more adventurous frame of mind there was also a supply of hang-gliding supplies, skydiving equipment, as well as tanks, rubber suits, and specialized gear for scuba divers.

But the owner of the store wasn't of much help. "We brought him in, all right," he said. "But I can't tell you much more than that."

Rick's eyebrows arched with an unspoken question.

"There isn't much more to tell," Kemper continued. "He didn't talk. Not a word the whole trip. Sat there with his eyes closed most of the time."

"Sleeping?"

"Naw. I think he just didn't want to talk."

Rick thought it was a pretty effective way of

cutting off conversation—and unwanted questions. It wasn't easy to keep talking to someone who wouldn't look at you, or even acknowledge that you were there.

"And when you landed," Rick prompted. "What happened then? He had a sprained ankle. Did anyone take him to the hospital?"

Rod Kemper gave that some thought while he rearranged a display of fishing lures. "No," he said finally, looking toward the door as a customer entered. "It's a funny thing, too. Seems to me one of the guys did offer him a ride."

"And he refused?"

"I guess you could say that he did." The store owner frowned over the memory. "He walked away. No answer. No comment. Not a word. We were standing around on the field. Someone said something about a ride. But he paid no attention. It was like he didn't even hear."

"I don't suppose anyone noticed where he went?"

Rod Kemper shook his head. "Not me. I really didn't pay much attention. There was no reason. He was just a hitchhiker. We picked him up. We gave him a ride. We dropped him off. We went our way. He went his. If he didn't want to talk— that was his problem. If he wanted to limp on a sprained ankle all the way into town, that was also his problem."

"Sure," Rick agreed as Kemper moved away to take care of a customer.

Marc picked up a baseball and rolled it around in his hand. "Doesn't help much, does it?"

Rick wasn't so sure. "Maybe not," he murmured. "But then, on the other hand, maybe we did learn something. Our hiker friend didn't talk about himself, didn't give his name, and didn't want a ride. It's all fitting into the same pattern. He didn't want his picture in the paper, either. For some reason he doesn't seem to want people to know who he is, where he is, or what he is doing. By refusing a ride he kept everyone from knowing where he was going."

Marc heaved a sigh. "Well, at least now we know this break-in wasn't connected to the plane crash."

"Seems like it," Rick agreed. "Only trouble is, now we have two questions. Why was our hiker afraid to be seen? And where is the missing pilot?"

Marc's shoulders sagged. As they talked, they left the store and began sauntering slowly back toward the Gazette building. As they passed a telephone booth, Rick stopped abruptly and stepped inside, dragging Marc after him.

"When you gave the information to the police last night, about the pilot, who'd you talk to?"

"Sergeant . . . somebody," Marc replied. "I didn't pay much attention to his name."

"Randall?"

Marc shrugged. "Could have been."

It would fit, Rick thought. Randall had been on duty later that same evening to investigate the Gazette break-in. It was worth a try anyway.

Sergeant Randall was out, but when Rick identified himself as being from the Gazette, the officer on duty was willing to pass along the information.

"There's not much to tell," he told Rick. And there wasn't. Only a post office box number—the same as Garrett had written on the aircraft rental form.

"We checked that out," the officer went on. "The box number is registered to someone named James Garrett. But that's about all the information they had on record, except that he pays for it every year in advance—in cash."

One more dead end.

"What about the credit card company?" Rick asked. "Wouldn't they have some record of where he worked? That's one of the standard questions on the application forms."

"You're right, it is. When Garrett applied for the card, he said he worked for some outfit over in Phoenix, Arizona, called Triple Sun Lasers. He was telling the truth. He did work for them. For about four months. Did some kind of specialized computer programming for them. No complaints. That was three years ago. No forwarding address."

"A similar job here maybe?"

The police officer groaned. "We thought of that. Have you any idea how many computer companies there are in this part of California. Not to mention electronics. We even have an outfit north of town that's big on lasers."

"Preston," Rick put in. Garrett had worked for a laser company in Arizona. It would make sense that he—

"They never heard of Garrett."

So much for that idea. But, he reasoned, that would have been too easy a connection. "How about the telephone number?"

"No help there, either. That belongs to a used-car lot on the north side of town. They never heard of anyone named Garrett."

"Interesting," Rick murmured.

"It is," the officer agreed. "And you can add this to the picture. The telephone company has no number in this town, or anywhere nearby—listed or unlisted—for anyone by that name."

Then it wasn't a simple explanation like a transposed number.

"You didn't happen to check for his driver's license?"

"We did," the police officer said with a tired laugh. "There are six or seven men named James Garrett driving cars in California, but not one of them lives anywhere near White Valley."

"What about a pilot's license?"

Rick could almost hear the officer shrug on the other end of the line. "Same story. Nobody by that name flies a plane and has an address within a hundred miles of here. We're checking them out. But. . . ." He let the rest of the sentence hang.

"Sounds like someone who has been covering his tracks pretty carefully."

"Our thoughts exactly." There was a pause on the other end of the line, and the sound of pages being turned. "Guess that's all we've got," the officer said. "Not much help, is it?"

"Not much," Rick agreed. Before hanging up he

passed along what little they had learned about the break-in at the Gazette.

"Gotcha," the police officer said. "I'll pass the word to Randall."

A call to the emergency clinic at White Valley Hospital didn't add any more information. Monday evening had been quiet—only a few minor accidents. Definitely no sprained ankles.

Rick leaned against the wall of the phone booth and squinted against the reflection of the late afternoon sun off a store window.

"He didn't go to the hospital?" Marc asked.

Rick shook his head.

"So maybe the sprain wasn't so serious."

Rick's thoughts leaped back to the mountain valley again, and the moment the hiker had appeared. He'd used a forked branch as a makeshift crutch. And he had been limping. That had been obvious. But. . . . His thoughts suddenly raced off in another direction.

"You just might have something there," Rick said quickly. "Maybe that sprain wasn't serious at all."

"What do you mean?"

"Maybe it wasn't even sprained."

"He faked it?"

"Can you think of a better way to drum up enough sympathy to get yourself a free ride?"

Marc gave Rick a long, thoughtful look. "I don't know," he said at last. "If he wasn't injured, why did he bother? He could have hiked out from there in less than a day."

"Unless he had a good reason to be in a hurry." There was that question of time again.

Marc made a face. "Hunger has made your mind weak," he said. "You're stretching for explanations. Why should he be in such a big hurry?"

"Why did he wipe his face from my pictures?" Rick retorted. "But you're right about one thing. I am hungry. Even more than I was an hour ago." He pushed off from the telephone booth.

A half hour later, after polishing off a large hamburger with everything, an order of French fries, two glasses of milk, plus a slab of blueberry pie with ice cream, he had to admit that he did feel better. He drained his glass, set it on the table and leaned back.

Midafternoon at Ernie's Restaurant was always quiet. Less than a dozen customers—mostly store clerks and office workers from the nearby government building—were dreamily sipping away their coffee breaks. No one seemed anxious to interrupt the mood and head back to work. Soft background music added to the relaxing atmosphere.

Rick watched idly as two salesmen pushed themselves up from stools at the counter and drifted toward the door. Somebody's coffee break was over. And—the door opened and another man came in—someone else's was just beginning.

Now there's someone who has come for more than a solo moment with a cup of coffee, Rick noted. The newcomer had paused not more than two steps from the door while his eyes made a quick survey of the room's occupants. Looking for someone.

The survey stopped at the boys' table. At that

same instant, Rick's mind snapped out of its fog as he recognized the newcomer. A dozen quick steps later Rod Kemper was standing next to them.

"Your office said I might find you here," Kemper told Rick. "Mind if I join you?"

"Not at all," Rick said. He waved to a chair, but the action was hardly necessary. Kemper had already seated himself and was leaning forward across the table. There was an intense, questioning look on his face.

"Something wrong?" Marc asked. The answer had to wait until the waitress took his coffee order.

"Do you remember the name of the guy who was piloting that plane that crashed? The one we found up in the mountains?" The store owner's eyes jumped from Rick to Marc and back again.

Rick nodded. "Garrett."

"James Garrett?"

Another nod.

"That's what I thought."

Rick studied Kemper's face briefly. "Do you know him?"

The owner of the sports shop shook his head. "In a way, you could say that." He spooned sugar into his coffee, stirred it, and took a sip. "A short time after you left the store this afternoon I was sorting through the charge card slips. We're supposed to take them in to the bank every couple of days. Have to if we want our money. But with all that happened—the crash and the search and everything—I was behind schedule. Know what I mean?"

Rick couldn't think of anything else to do except nod his head one more time.

"So while things were quiet I was trying to get the receipts in order. People use all kinds of cards these days—MasterCard, Visa, American Express. They all have to go to different banks. So they all have to be sorted and put in order."

Rick tried to look sympathetic, rather than impatient. Some people had a compulsion to give every little detail when they told a story. It was tempting to blurt out, "Get to the point!" but he resisted the urge. This was a story the store owner would have to tell at his own pace.

Kemper took another mouthful of coffee and set the cup back on the table. "I had forgotten all about him until I came across the name on one of the slips. And then I wasn't real sure."

"Sure about what?" Rick prompted.

"Garrett. He was in the store last week. Friday."

Rick's eyes met Marc's briefly before he looked back at the owner of the sports shop. "It could have been someone else with the same name."

"No." Kemper pulled a familiar slip of paper from his pocket and waved it. A duplicate charge card receipt. "James Garrett. The same one."

"But—" Rick stopped. "How can you be sure?"

Kemper dropped the receipt onto the table.

"He bought a parachute."

E I G H T
THE PARACHUTE

A parachute?

Rick frowned over the word. Why did Kemper seem to think that information was significant? What was so important about a parachute? Didn't every small plane have one? Wasn't there some kind of rule about things like that? Just like cars were supposed to be equipped with seat belts, and ships had lifeboats, and the big jets that flew over the ocean had life jackets for each passenger. It seemed like a parachute should be a normal piece of safety equipment in a small plane, but Rick wasn't sure. As he had admitted to Marc earlier, he didn't know much about planes and flying.

Then suddenly it all came clear.

"A parachute!" he exclaimed. "Of course."

That's why they had found no sign of the pilot in the plane. He wasn't there because he had jumped. He'd bailed out well before the crash.

And that opened up a jumbo assortment of possibilities and questions.

"But not any ordinary chute," Kemper said, placing his coffee cup on the table. He pointed to the charge card receipt. "See that number?"

Rick picked up the small slip of paper, glanced briefly at the date and the name JAMES GARRETT, then ran his eyes down to the space reserved for entering a customer's purchases. There was only one item there—a number followed by the word "Parachute," and in the space to the right of that, the purchase price. The number was obviously too short to be a serial number.

"What's it mean?"

"That's a special model," Kemper said eagerly. "An XL Cloud. A sky diver's chute."

"Sky diver?" Marc repeated. "You figure Garrett jumped when the plane got into trouble?"

"I don't know about the plane getting into trouble," Kemper answered. "I don't even know for sure that he jumped. But I'll tell you one thing. He didn't buy that chute for emergency use, like a guy who owns a boat might buy a life jacket. What he bought the day before that flight was a first-line tournament chute. With that XL Cloud you don't just float down, you fly it to your target almost like a glider. And any guy who knows enough to buy a chute like that knows how to use it, and also knows well enough when and how to jump from a plane."

Rick remembered an air show he had attended and photographed for the Gazette the previous summer. There had been sky divers there, jumping out at several thousand feet and free-falling for what seemed like forever before opening their chutes. Then they had put on a spectacular display of controlled flight by parachute, finishing up when they landed with amazing accuracy on what was really a very small target.

And that was the kind of chute the missing pilot had purchased?

"Could be he was an amateur who had read

some good books," Marc suggested. "Maybe someone recommended that number to him as a good model."

Kemper shook his head quickly. "No," he said. "He was no amateur. I'll guarantee that. I've sold my share of parachutes to a lot of different people. Some of them were newcomers to the sport. But not this guy Garrett. I could tell he had experience. He wasn't interested in anything except that model. He could have bought a cheaper type of parachute. One that would have landed him safely. But he wasn't interested. He wanted this model, and nothing else. If I hadn't one in stock he'd have gone someplace else. He knew what he wanted. He asked questions like a pro. And when he examined that chute, he handled it like a pro."

As if in a daze, Marc reached for the charge card receipt, glanced at it and slowly placed it back on the table. "What difference does it make what kind of parachute he bought? He—" His eyes widened and extra gravity suddenly took hold of his lower jaw. "He bought that the day before the flight?"

"That's right," Kemper said. "On Friday."

"But. . . ." Marc stammered. "That makes it sound like Garrett knew in advance he was going to crash."

The implications had taken a little longer for Marc to grasp. But then, Rick reasoned, the helicopter pilot didn't appear to have what anyone would call a suspicious mind.

Kemper nodded his head slowly, seriously. "It

does make you wonder, doesn't it? Mind you, I'm not making any accusations. We don't even know that he had the chute with him when he took off." He paused, looking thoughtful.

Rick nodded his head slowly in agreement. "Can you remember enough about Garrett to describe him?"

Kemper's eyes narrowed in thought. "Not much," he said. "I'd say he could be in his late twenties—maybe two or three years more than that. About average height. Average build. Can't describe his eyes. He was wearing sunglasses. Can't describe his face either. But I sure wouldn't forget it."

"Why's that?"

"His beard," Kemper said. "I haven't seen a full beard like that in years. No way to tell what his features were underneath all that fur."

Marc's attention suddenly sharpened. "A beard?"

"Right." Kemper's hand's came up, forming a cup around his chin, but inches away from his face. "Big, like this. Bushy. Reddish brown. Know what I mean?"

Marc nodded. There was a thoughtful expression on his face as he looked away to the window.

Kemper chuckled. "I remember thinking that he was one guy who could bail out in cold weather and not worry about his face freezing on him."

Rick got the picture. He looked over at Marc, but the young pilot didn't seem to be listening. He was lost in thoughts of his own.

"He said he had some kind of high-tech job and he liked skydiving for relaxation." Kemper laughed lightly.

"You mean high-tech like computers and electronics and that kind of stuff?"

"I suppose. Those were his words, not mine."

Rick shrugged. There was no surprise in that. They already knew much about Garrett. Besides, electronics was big business in central California. Everything from video games to computers to companies that were doing special work for the government. Even around a small town like White Valley there were at least three such companies that he knew of. His father's was one of them.

"Garrett said he liked skydiving because it helped him to escape from pressure and tension." Kemper shook his head. "Everyone to their own form of insanity, I guess. For myself, now, when I like to relax I like to sit on the edge of a stream and drown worms."

"Me too," Rick agreed. He couldn't imagine anything relaxing about stepping out of a plane at several thousand feet.

The owner of the sports shop pushed his chair back from the table and stood up. "Gotta get back to the store." He waved at the receipt. "That's my file copy. I'll need it back some time. But you can hang onto it for a few days if you think it's any help. It might not mean anything. Might be a coincidence." He moved toward the door. "Let me know if anything turns up."

Marc let out a heavy sigh as the restaurant door closed behind Kemper, and allowed himself to

slide low in his seat. For a time he was silent,
absentmindedly watching his finger tracing
imaginary aimless circles on the tabletop.

"Something on your mind?" Rick asked.
"Something Kemper said?"

Marc shook his head.

Rick studied him briefly, frowned slightly, then
looked out the window. He pictured the rugged
mountain valleys he had flown over yesterday.

There had been no emergency messages before
the crash saying the plane was in trouble. At what
point over those mountains had Garrett bailed
out? How far had the plane flown without anyone
at the controls? How far could it fly? The wind
and air currents would probably affect that as
much as anything. Had the Cessna circled, or
flown in a straight line? From what direction?

Rick's shoulders sagged. If Garrett had landed
up there, it would take weeks to cover all the
possible country. By that time—

"You really think that's how it happened?" Marc
asked softly. "You think Garrett jumped?"

"It sure would answer a few questions."

"I suppose. . . ."

"Didn't your cousin say someone had tampered
with the controls?" Rick reminded.

"Yeah. He said I did it." Marc scowled. "But I
figure he was just making that up as a good excuse to get me out of his hair."

Was that all it was? Rick's mind leaped back to
the early afternoon encounter with Sam Blair. A
family personality clash might be part of it, all
right. And yet. . . . His eyes narrowed thought-

fully. Somehow, he couldn't see the explanation being quite that simple. But then again, he didn't know Marc's cousin all that well.

Rick picked up a spoon and absentmindedly tapped it against the table. "Try this idea on for size," he suggested. "Garrett, for some unknown reason, wants to disappear—really drop out of sight. He wants everyone to think he has been killed in a plane crash. So he charters a small plane and says he's going to fly over the mountains to Nevada. He rigs the plane to crash someplace up there—" He frowned over that thought. "Would that be hard to set up?"

Marc shook his head. "Not if he knew what he was doing. The easiest way, I suppose, would be to kill the engine and let it go until it lost flying speed. Eventually it would have to hit the ground. Or he could even cut the throttle way back so that the prop was barely turning. Same result."

Rick nodded. That was about how he had calculated it. Up in that country there wouldn't be much danger of anyone else getting hurt in the process. No towns. Except for an occasional cabin, there was scarcely a building of any kind.

"So," Rick went on, "he sets the plane to crash someplace up there in the mountains and he jumps out. It's about as good a place as any to pull a vanishing act."

"I don't know," Marc said doubtfully. "It's rugged country. A man could get hurt pretty easy up there, especially dropping in by parachute. Crazy air currents could smack him against a rock cliff. Or hang him up in some tall trees."

"But," Rick pointed out, "Garrett likely knew all that. And he knew how to handle those problems if they came up. Remember that tournament sky diver's chute he bought. Those things can be controlled and directed, almost like flying a glider."

"OK," Marc agreed slowly. "So maybe it's possible. But if he wanted people to believe he had been killed, he blew it. There was no fire after the crash to wipe out evidence. You said yourself that if anyone had been in that plane when it crashed, they'd still be there."

"That's the problem with tricky plans. There's always a chance something won't work out according to the figuring. After all with half a tank of fuel left, anyone would expect the Cessna would burn on impact. I sure would."

"But it didn't."

"Right." Rick agreed. "He missed some little technicality. The tank didn't rupture. There was no spark. The plane somehow skimmed the tree tops when it came in—maybe one of those tricky air currents again. So instead of smacking head-on into the side of a mountain, it made a belly landing on a talus slope. There's such a small chance of something like that happening . . . you can't even say he miscalculated. It was just one of those things. And if it hadn't ended up the way it did, who knows how long it might have been before anyone became suspicious."

Marc sighed. "That's the problem. It's only a suspicion. We can't prove anything. Just because Garrett bought a parachute—even a special one—doesn't mean that he had it with him on that flight. Or that he used it. All we know for sure is that the plane crashed, and the pilot—some guy named James Garrett—is missing. Like your hiker friend who broke into your darkroom, he's a missing face. The only difference is that we have a name to tag onto one of them, for all the good that does."

Rick nodded. The missing pilot seemed to be as illusive as the injured hiker. Unless someone happened to turn up the parachute in the bush someplace, or unless Garrett himself was found, all they would ever have out of this story was suspicions.

Everything seemed to point to the fact that Garrett had carefully planned his disappearance. He certainly wouldn't have left the parachute lying around where it could be easily found. He would have disposed of it somehow. As for Garrett himself, he'd be miles away by now—in another state, down in Mexico, or even in Canada.

Rick sighed. "Maybe we can get Sam to listen to our ideas," he suggested. "Maybe he'll at least let you have your job back."

Marc snorted. "That shows how much you know about Sam Blair."

"I just—" Rick began.

"You're fooled, like I was, because he goes to church. You still think that might make a difference." The young helicopter pilot's lips pressed together hard for a moment. "Well, let me tell you something about Sam Blair. What you saw out there today was the real Sam Blair. For him, lately, that's normal."

"Lately?"

"Yeah. When I first moved here from Oregon, about a year ago, he only acted like that once in awhile. Monday for him wasn't so much different from Sunday—just enough so you could notice. But the last few months it's been happening like that just about every day."

"What's bothering him?"

"Me," Marc growled. "He wants me out of there."

"Why?"

Marc's shoulders lifted in a shrug.

"If he doesn't want you around, why doesn't he just fire you?"

A strange grin flickered across Marc's lips. "My father set him up in that business. Loaned him the money and made things easy for him until things got going."

"And I'll bet he still owes your dad a good chunk of that money."

"Exactly," Marc said. "That's why he won't kick me out unless he can find a good excuse."

A puzzled frown made grooves in Rick's forehead. "You're a good pilot. Why should he want you out of there?"

"He's got his reasons."

Rick supposed there could be a lot more to the story than Marc was telling.

"One thing you can count on for sure about Sam Blair," Marc went on. "He'll work any angle that he figures is to his advantage."

"A lot of people are like that," said Rick. "Just when you think you can count on them, just when you think you've got their reputation figured out, they go and do something to disappoint you or hurt you."

"And how many of them go to church?"

There's the bottom line, Rick thought. *That's what's really bothering him. He wants to believe there's something genuine there.*

"Quite a few, I guess," he conceded.

Marc snorted.

"Don't write us all off because of one bad example."

Marc looked blank for a moment. "You—?"

Rick nodded.

" . . . and your uncle, too. I should have known." Marc shook his head sheepishly. "Boy, I sure put my foot in my mouth that time."

Rick grinned.

"I'm sorry," Marc said. "I didn't mean. . . . You're not the same. . . ."

"That's encouraging."

"I mean it."

Rick took a deep breath, his mind racing. "Church isn't what makes the difference," he said, at last. "It's God. A Christian—a real one—is someone who is willing to let God make him different." He paused. "That's part of it anyway."

Marc said nothing.

In the silence that stretched between them, the waitress came with their bill, took their money, and eventually brought back their change.

"You really believe that, don't you," Marc said at last, his voice barely above a whisper.

Rick nodded.

Another minute or two slid by without a word.

"You could be right," Marc murmured. He pushed his chair back and slowly got to his feet. "That could be the reason. You're different, anyway."

Rick stood up and started for the door. There were so many things he would like to say. But maybe it wasn't the right time. For now, maybe it was enough that Marc had noticed and that he was thinking about it.

At the door he stepped aside for an incoming customer. As he did so, his eye caught the pile of newspapers on the counter. A familiar picture filled most of the top half of page one. The Gazette's evening edition was already on the streets.

Marc saw it at the same instant. "Did you give Sam a copy of that shot?"

Rick glanced back and nodded. "I think so. Why?"

"No special reason."

It wasn't until they were out on the street and a half block closer to the newspaper building that Rick realized what Marc's question meant. Those pictures he had printed up for Sam Blair . . . five of them. And one of them, he was sure, had been the shot that showed the group of searchers scattered across the slope near the wreck. The picture that had been printed before the negative was doctored. The one that showed the searchers and—

Rick swung around so abruptly that Marc jumped to one side, startled.

"Those pictures," he said. "What would Sam have done with them?"

Marc blinked back his surprise. He thought for a minute before saying, "No idea."

"Would he still have them at his office at the airport?"

"I guess. If he didn't throw them away."

"Would he do that?"

"Sure. The mood he was in, he just might." Marc cocked his head. "Why the sudden interest?"

Rick explained. "I should have remembered." He began walking again, a little faster now. "You game to give it a try?"

Marc looked thoughtful for a moment. "Why not." There was a touch of mischief in the grin that accompanied his answer.

Perhaps it was the sudden feeling of making progress after so many dead ends that made Rick's feet feel lighter as they sprinted for the Gazette parking lot. Even his old car seemed to sense the mood. It started without a protest, for a change.

It wasn't much—that picture—but it was something. A chance to bring at least one of the missing faces out where they could see it.

The mood lasted all the way to the airport, where Sam Blair quickly put an end to it. "What are you doing here?" he growled.

Rick wasn't too sure if the question was aimed at Marc or him.

"Those pictures I gave you," Rick said. "One of my negatives was damaged after I made those prints. I was wondering—"

Sam Blair didn't let him finish. "Over there," he snapped, waving a hand in the general direction of a small steel desk in the corner of the office. "I haven't had time to look at them. Got work to do." Then, as if that explained his actions, he abruptly stepped through the door that led into the workshop.

Marc rolled his eyes. "He's really glad to see me," he whispered.

"I can tell."

There was the muted sound of an argument from the other side of the door. Two voices. Short angry bursts of words. The boys couldn't actually hear what was being said, but Rick thought the tone was right in character for Sam Blair.

There was something vaguely familiar about the second voice. But Rick couldn't hear it clearly enough to be sure.

Then the sharp voices abruptly stopped. Whatever the argument had been about, someone had won. Rick shrugged as he crossed to the desk, picked up the familiar brown envelope, and turned it over. His hand froze momentarily in midair.

The envelope was open—sliced neatly with a knife or letter opener. Rick tipped the brown folder, allowing the prints to slide out onto the desk. Four of them. Four pictures of the battered body of a little Cessna 172.

Four. Not five.

"One's missing," he breathed. He shuffled the four prints around on the desk, then slowly raised his eyes until they met Marc's.

"You're sure," the pilot protested. "Perhaps you didn't count—"

"There were five," Rick insisted. "I'm positive." He fingered the open edge of the envelope. It had been sealed when he delivered it. "And you can guess which picture is missing."

Marc's eyes widened.

At that instant the workshop door opened a few inches. There was a brief scuffing sound, then the door slammed shut again. Rick swung around, his muscles tensing in preparation for another explosion of angry words from Sam Blair.

But the door remained closed. There was the sound of something being dragged across the floor, and then a sharp thump as the object was pushed up against the door from the other side.

More voices, still muffled by the thickness of the door and walls. But not so muffled that they couldn't tell that the last phrase was a sharply spoken, angry command.

That last voice wasn't Sam Blair's.

"What's happening?" Marc looked worried.

Rick didn't blame him. He was getting a strange, uneasy feeling himself.

"I don't know," he said. "But I think we'd better find out."

Was that the sound of running footsteps across a concrete floor?

Rick leaped for the door handle, turned it, and drove his shoulder against the panel. It only moved about an inch. Whatever had been pushed against the door from the other side—a cupboard or a crate or something—was holding it firm.

"Together," Rick said.

Marc added his 180 pounds to the effort.

There was a loud grating sound and the crack between the door and the frame widened to a little more than a foot.

"Again."

More movement. Another foot.

There was no reaction from the room beyond. But then Rick hadn't really expected one. Those running footsteps he'd heard. . . .

Cautiously he squeezed through the crack. One quick glance confirmed that the room was empty.

"They're gone."

Marc was barely a second behind him as they raced for the big door that opened from the workshop onto the concrete airport pavement.

"There they are!" Marc whispered loudly.

Two men were halfway to the helicopter pad. Running. One was Sam Blair. He was easy to recognize. The other one. . . .

Running with a limp? A sore leg? A mountain-climbing injury? Or a. . . ?

The second man turned to look over his shoulder. As he did so, something fell from inside his windbreaker. In his hurry, he didn't seem to notice. From a distance the object looked like a piece of paper. Or perhaps a small brown envelope.

For Rick, that one glimpse was enough. He'd seen that face before. The scene was vivid on the full-color wide-screen of his mind. That high mountain valley. The men coming out of the woods. And one extra man—looking for a free ride back to civilization. He'd been limping then, too, leaning on a makeshift crutch.

Suddenly it all came together, and the missing face had a name.

There wasn't time to think about what the man might have dropped in his hurry. The sight of a gun lifting to point at them sent the boys diving for cover before the thought could even complete itself.

"That's Garrett!" Rick yelled.

A hastily fired shot put an effective exclamation mark on the end of the announcement. The bullet kissed the edge of the building and whined off across the runway.

N I N E
THE CHASE

Rick edged carefully toward the big outside doors. His back was pressed to the wall. Garrett's shot hadn't come anywhere close to them, but that didn't stop the strange sensation that rippled and tingled across the nerves in the back of his neck.

His mouth suddenly felt dry.

"Can you see them?" Marc was hugging the opposite wall.

Rick licked his lips and slid sideways until his eyes cleared the opening.

Nothing.

Another six inches.

There they were. Sam Blair and Garrett had reached one of the helicopters. Sam was already in the pilot seat. Garrett, still holding the gun, was clambering in beside him.

Rick waved Marc forward, and at that moment the big rotors began to turn.

The helicopter motor was roaring at full power as they sprinted into the open. They were just in time to see the blue, white, and orange Bell Jet Ranger lift from the pad and swing away, nose down, across the airport. The strong down-draft cleared the landing pad of sand and papers. The sand settled back down immediately, leaving a wisp of dust in the air. The papers fluttered and tumbled for a moment or two before they too dropped back to the pavement.

For just an instant Rick thought he saw Garrett look back at the blowing paper. And then they were gone.

East, he noted. They were going east. Toward the mountains. Instinctively he began to run toward the second Bell Jet Ranger. If they took off immediately they could keep the other craft in sight. It they. . . .

Rick had covered about thirty feet before he realized he was alone. When he slowed and turned, he found Marc hadn't moved. He was still standing by the workshop door, as if he was glued to the pavement. His eyes were on the rapidly departing helicopter. Confusion twisted at his face.

"Come on," Rick called. "Garrett's getting away."

As if in a dream, Marc slowly turned. "Garrett?" he repeated. "The same Garrett from the plane?"

"The same one," Rick said. "The same Garrett who parachuted down into the mountains. The same Garrett who injured himself and begged a ride back to town with the search party. The same Garrett who removed his face from my photograph. The same—"

He broke off as Marc began to walk toward him.

"The same. . . ?" Marc said. "You're sure?"

"As sure as I can be," Rick told him. "I know he's the hiker we brought back. He said he'd sprained his ankle, but he didn't say how it happened. Maybe he tripped on something along the trail. That's rugged country. On the other hand, he could also have sprained his ankle when he made a bad landing, because of one of those tricky air currents. Even the experts sometimes have accidents."

"But the beard," Marc said. "Kemper said Garrett had a beard."

"A razor would take care of that in short order," Rick pointed out. "That's no problem. As a matter of fact, if Garrett was trying to disappear by pulling that stunt with the plane and the parachute, the beard would be just one more item that he would attend to. What better way to change his appearance than by shaving off a full beard?"

"But. . . ." Marc's voice trailed off uncertainly.

"Look," Rick said. "It doesn't matter at the moment what his name is. He has a gun. And he has Sam. If we take off now, we'll have half a chance of keeping them in sight. At the same time we can radio the police."

Marc still looked unsure as he began to move, not very quickly, toward the helicopter pad.

What was the matter with him, anyway, Rick fumed to himself. The pilot seemed to be more concerned over Garrett's identity than he was about the fact that his cousin had been forced, at gunpoint, to fly the helicopter. Had his loyalty to his cousin faded that much already?

Rick could still faintly hear the sound of Sam Blair's helicopter. It was fading fast with distance. From ground level it was already out of sight.

At the landing pad, Marc fumbled through his pockets for several long seconds, searching for the key. By the time it appeared in his hand, Rick was finding it virtually impossible to control his rising impatience. It almost appeared as though Marc was deliberately stalling.

A brown envelope lying on the pavement nearby caught Rick's attention. Was that what Garrett had dropped when he looked back?

It appeared to be an ordinary item—just a plain 6-by-10-inch manila envelope, like many he had seen around the mail room at the Gazette. What did catch his attention was the slight bulge in the paper, as though there were something inside.

It couldn't be important, he told himself. Thousands of envelopes just like that one were stuffed into mailboxes every day. Most of them contained some kind of printed matter. Even someone like Garrett likely received junk mail.

Yet as his hand touched the door handle to the helicopter, he hesitated and looked back at the brown rectangle one more time.

Brett Shannon had told him once that there was a fine line between plain nosiness and a newsman's curiosity. At the moment, he wasn't sure which of those was pulling his attention back to the envelope.

Marc was taking his place at the controls when Rick's curiosity got the best of him. A quick jump, a half dozen steps there, and a half dozen back again.

There was something in the envelope, Rick noted as he strapped himself in. Something square, about the thickness of a thin piece of cardboard. When he flipped it over, he found only an insignia printed in blue where the return address would normally be in the upper left-hand corner. No name. No address. Just a space-age letter P.

It looked familiar. He was sure he'd seen that insignia before somewhere.

Where?

Marc shot him a curious glance as the motor came to life. "Do you always pick up garbage?"

Rick shook his head. "Garrett dropped it."

"You really figure Garrett and that hiker are the same person?"

"Yeah," Rick said. "I do." He opened the envelope and upended it so that the item inside slid out into his hand. "And this makes me certain I'm right."

He held up a small square open-topped blue envelope about 5½ inches wide. Inside that envelope was another square—black this time—enough smaller so that it fit snugly into the folder.

"What is it?"

Rick held it up, and turned it slowly. "That, my friend, is a computer disk. Or if you want to be really precise, a floppy diskette."

Marc's hand tensed on the controls. "Computer disk?" he repeated. "Garrett dropped it?"

"Exactly," Rick said. "And the police said that Garrett was into computers back in Arizona."

For the space of a dozen heartbeats Marc could only stare. First at Rick, then at the computer disk in his hand. "Then Garrett is—"

"—the hiker," Rick finished.

Marc reached over and took the brown envelope from his lap. He jabbed a finger at the insignia. "What's he doing with an envelope from Preston?"

Now it was Rick's turn to stare. "Preston?" he echoed. Of course. That's where he had seen that marking. Preston Laser-Optics! A dozen more pieces of the puzzle suddenly fell into place.

What was someone like Garrett doing with a computer disk from Preston? They'd told the police they had never heard of Garrett.

Suddenly he remembered the laser weapons testing Brett Shannon had mentioned. Preston did a lot of top secret research work for the government. Was that one of their projects? At that thought he could almost feel the contents of the disk tingling in his hand.

"Lasers," Marc repeated. "That outfit Garrett worked for in Arizona was into lasers, too. And computers."

"Yeah," Rick said. "Lasers. Computers. And Garrett."

Abruptly Marc whirled in his seat and jerked savagely at the controls. The helicopter leaped into the air from its landing pad. At the same time the pilot's fingers squeezed down on the radio control button and he began to talk rapidly into his microphone. Rick couldn't hear what he was saying, but he guessed the radio was set to a police frequency.

The airport was almost out of sight behind them before Rick felt it was safe to ease up on his white-knuckled grip on the edge of his seat. Judging by the sound of the motor and by the way the ground was racing by beneath them, Marc was pushing the Bell Jet Ranger to its limits. And he wasn't wasting any more precious seconds in climbing for altitude. Whatever had caused his hesitation earlier wasn't there now.

"Do you know where you're going?"

Marc Blair's lips pressed together hard for a moment, forming a thin, grim line. "I think so," he said at last. He jerked his head toward a map pocket nestled between the seats. "That chart. The top one. Open it up."

Rick spread it open on his lap.

"Run your finger along a line from the airport to that valley in the mountains where we found the plane."

Rick did as he was directed.

"Right about there," Marc said. "*If* you're right. *If* Garrett did rig that Cessna for a disappearing act, and *if* he really jumped, then he had to be aiming for someplace in that area."

Rick studied the map. It was as good a guess as any. There was no telling how far the wind currents might have blown Garrett from his intended landing spot. But it was a place to start. And if they could catch sight of the other helicopter up there somewhere. . . .

"What's on that disk?" Marc asked.

Rick picked up the computer disk again and turned it over in his hand. "Could be just about anything," he said. "Only a computer programmed to read this disk could tell us that." He pulled the disk out of its protective envelope, examined it briefly, then slipped it back. "One of these disks, recorded on both sides like this one, could hold maybe 180 or 200 close-packed pages of information. And this is a small one."

The expression on Marc's face and the shrill whistle that rattled his headphones told Rick there was no need to say more. The possibilities that formed in his own mind made a rather dramatic picture. Two hundred pages of information, special computer programs, formulas, or designs and plans from a top secret laser research center.

"And Sam's mixed up in a deal like that?" Even on the headphones there was no mistaking the sound of stunned shock in Marc's voice.

"What. . . ?" Rick turned. What was he saying? That he thought Sam had something to do with stealing information from Preston?

"Sam was forced to take Garrett up in the helicopter," Rick reminded. "You saw the gun."

"Maybe," Marc said. "And maybe that was an act for our benefit."

Furrows formed on Rick's forehead as he studied his companion. His mind raced back over the minutes since they had stepped into the Blair Aviation office. Had he missed something? Had Marc caught a word or two from those muffled voices in the other room? No, that wasn't possible. Anything Marc might have heard he would have caught himself.

They were beginning the climb into the high mountains when Marc finally spoke again.

"Sam knew him." Now he sounded bitter and discouraged.

"Knew who? Garrett?"

Marc nodded. "It was the beard that tipped me off," he said. "Garrett was out at the airport to see Sam about a week or ten days ago. I was working in the shop, so I didn't see them up close, except for a glimpse of the beard going by the hangar window. But I heard them." He sucked on his lower lip. "They talked about him taking up one of the planes."

"What's wrong with that?" Rick wanted to know. "If he was going to charter a plane for Saturday, it would make sense that he would plan ahead."

"Sure," Marc agreed. "Except that they talked like two guys who hadn't seen each other for a long time." As he spoke, he pulled back on the control to send the Bell Jet Ranger skimming up the side of a long wooded slope.

"You're sure it was Garrett?" Rick pressed. "There are plenty of beards around."

"Sam didn't actually say his name, but it was Garrett. I'm sure. He even talked about how he was working for Preston. And how surprised they were going to be when he didn't turn up for work."

Now it was Rick's turn to show shock. "He said all this to Sam?"

Marc nodded wordlessly.

Rick turned away and stared out at the hillside passing beneath them. The owner of the charter service had been uptight the day he came back from the scene of the crash. It was he who had suggested that the plane had been sabotaged. Was that because he knew it was going to be discovered? Was he trying to plant a seed of blame to take the suspicion away from himself? And away from Garrett?

Would he really do that to his own cousin?

Rick shook his head. Was Sam's churchgoing really just an act, as Marc suspected? Was there anything real in it? Did it mean anything to him at all? Or was it all a performance to make him appear more respectable to some people that he wanted to impress?

In his few contacts with him, Sam Blair certainly had done nothing to make himself likeable. Yet as crabby and obnoxious as Sam was, Rick couldn't bring himself to accept the story that Marc's cousin might be mixed up in any kind of scheme to steal computer data from a top secret research lab. There had to be some other explanation.

"We should be getting close." Marc's voice in the headphones interrupted Rick's thoughts.

"We're probably right on the flight path Garrett would have followed on Saturday," Marc explained. "Assuming he flew directly from White Valley." He shrugged. "If he went someplace else first—like Sacramento—then he would have come into the mountains from a whole lot farther north."

Rick leaned forward, his eyes probing for some sign of the other helicopter. He couldn't get out of his mind the description of Garrett that the police had given him. He was a man who seemed to be careful to cover his tracks. Everything he did pointed to that fact. Including removing himself from a routine newspaper photograph. Not just stealing the negative—that would have quickly attracted attention.

How far would he go to cover his tracks? How far would he go to be certain that his travels couldn't be traced?

What about Sam? If he wasn't involved—or even if he was—what would Garrett do with him?

Rick rubbed at his forehead as though trying to squeeze that thought out of his mind.

No flashes of blue or orange or white broke the color pattern of brown, green, and gray beneath them. No helicopter. Only rocks and trees. Just like the other day when they had spent an entire morning and afternoon scanning mountain country like this for the wrecked plane. His eyes began to throb with the memory of that search.

They skimmed across a ridge and then spun up and around in a tight, climbing curve.

Nothing. Nothing at all. Only rocky ridges splattered with patches of pine.

Why would anyone like Garrett want to come up here in the first place? If it was part of his elaborate escape plan to parachute down into some specific place in this rugged country, what did he have in mind?

He voiced his question to Marc, but the pilot only shook his head. "You're the newsman," he said. "You guys are all supposed to be part detective aren't you?"

Rick laughed. "That's what the editors figure, I guess."

They crossed another valley and climbed the

ridge beyond it, working their way up toward the higher peaks.

Everywhere he looked, it was the same. No helicopter. No people. Not even an old cabin.

There were only two possibilities, Rick thought. Either Garrett had some kind of hideout up here—some place safe and well hidden—or else he had another way of leaving the area. A simple hideout didn't seem likely. A man who was smart enough to lift important information out of a computer wasn't going to hide away like a hermit in a mountain cave or a cabin. He was going to go someplace where he could turn that information into money.

Where? And how would he get out of the mountains?

They climbed up over a higher ridge. Marc cut back their speed.

"There she is," the pilot announced suddenly. He nodded toward a small clearing on the north side of the ridge.

Rick's eyes followed the pointing figure. It wasn't possible. It couldn't be. Not this soon. They had practically flown directly to the spot. No hours of searching up and down valleys and canyons as they had done for the wrecked Cessna.

But there it was, on the far side of a rugged ridge, and above what looked like a long, narrow, deep canyon.

Even with the low angle of the sun, and the heavy shade in the clearing, there was no mistaking the blue, orange, and white coloring of the Blair helicopter.

"And there's why he came," Rick exclaimed an instant later. He pointed down into the canyon where a vehicle of some kind was half hidden by brush.

"A jeep?" Marc said. "He came up here for a jeep?" He kicked the Bell Jet Ranger around in a circle for a better look.

"It makes sense," Rick said. "Garrett planned on crashing the plane so that everyone would think he had been killed up there. Instead, he would parachute down unnoticed, climb into his jeep, and drive away. By the time the crash was discovered, who would remember seeing a nature lover, complete with camera, driving along a forest service road in an old jeep?"

Marc took another look at the hidden vehicle. "If that's true, Garrett has a problem, because now we've seen it. And if your guess is right, we have at least part of his plan figured out."

"Don't forget Sam," Rick said. "He knows what's happening, too."

Marc's fading loyalty to his cousin showed in the expression that flashed across his face. "Sam wouldn't tell. Not if he's in on the setup."

"Maybe he isn't," Rick said. The helicopter had drifted over the clearing in which its twin was resting. "Look!"

There was a figure on the ground near the front of the craft below them. Rick grabbed for the binoculars and focused.

"It's Sam."

The owner of Blair Aviation was seated on the ground, his back to the landing gear struts. There was something strange and unnatural about his position. As Rick twisted the focus knob he saw the reason. Sam Blair's hands were behind his back, around the strut. A glint of metal around his wrist showed as Sam shifted position.

"Garrett's handcuffed him to the helicopter," Rick reported.

"What?" Marc leaned forward to see for himself. "That could be part of their act, too. Like Garrett holding the gun on him back in the office."

Marc wasn't about to cut loose from that idea without some proof.

Rick pulled his gaze away from the grounded helicopter. "Speaking of Garrett, where is he?"

As if in answer to his question, there was a flash of flame from the shadow of the trees at the edge of the ridge. An instant later a starred crack flared in the window next to Rick's right ear.

"He's shooting at us," Marc shouted. He twisted the controls and sent the Bell Jet Ranger clawing for altitude.

Rick's lower jaw sagged as he stared at the crack.

It was close. No more that eight inches from his head.

T E N
BOX CANYON SHOWDOWN

"He's getting away!"

Marc's sharp exclamation jerked Rick's mind out of the daze it had fallen into at the sight of the crack left by the bullet.

Garrett was in the clear now, as he scrambled over the rocky ridge. He paused briefly before he jumped down to a narrow ledge a few feet below the top. Then it was a dusty slide down a long, steep dirt slope. He caught himself on a scrub pine, glanced up at the hovering helicopter, then plunged on down into the canyon.

Panic showed in every frantic movement.

"It'll take him at least another two or three minutes to reach the jeep," Rick said. "If he doesn't break a leg first."

"We can't do anything about that. We can't stop him. Not while he's got that gun." Marc backed the helicopter away from the ridge so that they had a clear view of Garrett's scrambling descent. "The best we can do is follow him until the law shows up."

"Then you did call the police?"

"As soon as we took off," Marc confirmed. He looked down through the window at his side. "He can still get away," he said. "If they don't get here before dark."

"Maybe." Rick absentmindedly picked up his Nikon, adjusted the zoom lens, focused on Garrett's frantic dash for freedom, and gently pressed the shutter release. He snapped his fingers as he lowered the camera. "We can't stop him, but maybe we can do something to slow him down."

Marc looked doubtful. "What do you have in mind?"

Rick studied the terrain beneath them. "That valley down there—that canyon—there's only one way out of it."

Marc leaned to one side and ran his eyes up and down the narrow valley. "You could be right, I suppose. How does that help?"

"Garrett could climb out of the top end on foot," Rick said. "But there's only one way out for the jeep. He has to go down. That makes it a good half mile before he's in the clear."

"So?" Marc left the one word question hanging.

"If we could get there first and block the canyon, he'd be boxed in."

Marc snorted. "Block it?" he echoed. "You've been watching too many of those fancy stunts on TV. Unless, of course you happen to have a case of dynamite in your back pocket."

Rick grinned a little sheepishly. "That did sound kind of dramatic, didn't it?" The idea was still good though. He was sure. Besides, what else could they do to stop Garrett? They didn't dare get too close to him while he still had that gun.

"I don't know what it's like down there," Rick admitted. "Or even if it is possible to do anything. And we don't have enough time to do anything really effective, like chopping down some trees across the road, or rolling down an assortment of large boulders, or—"

"Hold it." As he spoke, Marc swung the helicopter around and headed it down canyon. "There might be a way."

Within seconds they passed the end of the rocky ridge and dropped into a cross valley. Playing with the rudder pedals, Marc kicked the Bell Jet Ranger's tail around until they were facing back up the canyon and only inches from the ground.

"There," Marc said. "That's where he has to come out."

A faint trace of tire tracks disappeared between a pair of large rocks. It was the narrow opening to the canyon. But what could they do about it?

"That's a perfect place," Rick agreed. "But what do we use for a barricade?" There was nothing in sight that looked moveable without the pocket full of explosives Marc had mentioned.

"This!"

The helicopter glided forward until it seemed to be almost pushing against the rocks that sat like giant gateposts on either side of the trail leading into the canyon. Another touch at the controls and the craft made a quarter turn, then gently settled to the ground.

Dust swirled up and around them in a choking cloud.

There was no way that Garrett's jeep was going to get out of that canyon now. Not without wings of its own.

The rotors were still gently swishing thirty seconds later when the boys made a running, knee-skinning dive into the shelter of a ragged pile of boulders about a hundred feet from the narrow mouth of the canyon.

They scarcely had time to turn and crouch against the back of a large slab of granite before they heard the sound of the jeep's motor. Judging by the sound, Garrett was pushing it hard.

He's going to be surprised, Rick told himself. The screeching grind of locked brakes a moment later confirmed that thought. A heavy cloud of brown dust swirled out of the gap between the rocks. Then the hood of the jeep skidded into view.

Rick couldn't see Garrett from where they were crouched. That meant he also could not see them. A metallic click announced the opening of a door. Then a half dozen quick gravel-crunching foot-steps. Garrett was out of the jeep, probably creeping forward for a better look. Rick could imagine his sharp brown eyes probing for an alternate escape route.

"Pretty clever!"

The shout came from the right. Somewhere over beyond the big gatepost rock on that side.

Another gravel sound, like a miniature rock slide. Garrett was moving again.

"It's not going to do you any good, you know," Garrett called.

It was tempting to shout something back at him. But that was exactly what was expected of them. A single word—any sound would do— would tell Garrett where they were hiding. For now, their best defense was silence. They knew where he was, but for all he knew they might be close enough to jump him if he stepped out of cover.

The gun barked just then. The bullet ricocheted from a rock and screamed off across the valley.

Rick winced. That was the kind of sound that made a person want to dig a deep hole or get up and run like crazy. Garrett had fired that shot at random, likely thinking it might flush them out of cover.

"Listen," Marc whispered. "Up in the sky."

Rick heard what had caught Marc's sensitive hearing. A faint motor noise with a distinctive *thump-thump* rhythm.

"Helicopter?" Rick breathed.

Marc nodded and whispered back, "Two of them."

Garrett also heard them. Two quick gunshots echoed from the canyon walls, and two more bullets kicked up dust, marking the spots where they struck. Neither was close.

"How many shots do you suppose he has left?"

"No idea," Marc said. "But I'm not going out there to find out."

At that instant Garrett burst out of cover and began a scrambling, jumping run along the far side of the canyon mouth. For about five seconds the helicopter hid him from the boys' view. When they next saw him, he was running across the fire road heading for the woods on the opposite side of the valley.

Rick leaned around the rock. "It's no good," he called to the running man. "You're wasting your time."

Without slowing, Garrett half turned and fired another shot in their direction.

"You dropped that envelope back at the airport," Rick called again. "The one with the computer disk."

Garrett's momentum carried him forward a dozen steps before he slowed and began slapping with his left hand at his jacket where the inside pocket would be. Then he reached up and ripped the zipper down so that he could pull the jacket open and look.

It wasn't there. Just as Rick had said.

He cursed and began to run again, turning his head to look back. Emotion twisted at his features. At that moment, not concentrating on the uneven ground, he tripped over a weather-bleached branch half buried in the dry soil. He fell roughly to the ground, one leg twisted awkwardly beneath him. He rolled over once, scrambled forward on all fours for six or eight feet, and then was up and running again. His limp was now much more noticeable.

Suddenly the sound of the helicopter motors was loud as the first of the state police aircraft swept around the side of the mountain across from them.

"Let him go," Marc yelled to Rick. "He can't get away now."

Rick nodded and stood up. It was all but over.

Garrett was still running down the center of the valley. But a police helicopter was sweeping after him.

The missing face had been found. And a whole lot more.

By ten o'clock that night, the mouth of the box canyon in the Sierra Nevadas was at least beginning to return to its normal quiet, deserted condition. Daylight had lasted just long enough for Rick to finish his film.

One police helicopter, with Garrett aboard in handcuffs, had already left. The second was warming up to follow.

"That about wraps it up," one of the state police officers said. "Except, of course, for the official statements we'll still need from you."

"Sure," Rick said. "We'll stop in tomorrow sometime." He looked up as a second officer, who had been talking quietly on the police radio, strolled in their direction.

"Preston sends their thanks," he told the boys. "If it hadn't been for you, Garrett likely would have gotten away with one of the biggest security breaks this state—maybe the country—has ever seen." He shrugged. "They still don't know what he got."

Marc looked up in surprise. "Can't they tell?"

"It's not like stealing a book, or even a file from a locked cabinet," Rick put in. "Garrett somehow got hold of the computer security code password. But he didn't do any damage when he got into the system. He only copied what he wanted from the computer memory onto the disk. He didn't leave any trail behind. No clues. And no way to trace him. If he hadn't been caught, there would be no way that anyone could know that any top secret information had been taken."

"Until it began showing up in some other company's developments," the police officer added,

"or in the weapons of some foreign and unfriend-
ly country."

"Was that Garrett's plan?"

"We don't know. Maybe we never will, if Garrett
doesn't talk."

Rick shook his head. "Garrett's pretty smart
with computers. And he's not so dumb with
photo equipment either. He covered his tracks
pretty well with that stunt he pulled in our darkroom."

"If that picture had been published, there's a
chance someone he worked with might have recognized him," the officer agreed.

"One thing puzzles me," Rick said. "With the
security clearance at Preston as tight as it is, how
did Garrett ever get a job in the first place?"

It was the state police officer's turn to shake his
head. "He was clean. No police record of any
kind. Not even a parking ticket."

"This was his first effort?" Marc questioned.

"The first he has been caught at it," the officer
said. "As far as we know. We'll see what happens
when he begins to feel the pressure of questioning. Guys like that sometimes feel compelled to
brag when they're finally brought in. They like to
make sure we all know how smart they really are,
and how much they got away with before we
stumbled onto them."

"You know," Rick put in, "Garrett's face didn't
make it into the papers. But the story of the plane
crash was there, as well as on the radio and
television. Garrett's name was given as the missing pilot. White Valley police even called Preston,

but they said they never heard of anyone by that name."

"Oh, didn't I tell you?" asked the officer who had been speaking on the police radio earlier. "Out at Preston he was known as Ted Baker. They saw the story of the crash, but the name Garrett meant nothing to them."

"Which is his real name?" Marc asked. "Or does he have a third one?"

The officer shook his head and shrugged.

"It's Garrett." Sam Blair, who had been standing by silently in the shadows all this time, stepped forward as he spoke. One of the state troopers earlier had cut him free and he had brought the second Blair helicopter down to the valley. "His real name is Garrett."

Rick and Marc and the two police officers turned in unison. Each showed surprise at the sudden statement.

"How do you know that?"

Sam Blair bit his lip as his eyes swept slowly around the little group. "We went to college together," he said.

"But you didn't say anything," Marc protested.

Sam looked at the ground for a moment or two before he allowed his gaze to meet his cousin's. "No, I guess I didn't."

The hard, biting tone was gone from Sam Blair's voice, Rick noted. When he spoke they almost had to strain to catch the words.

"You knew he'd deliberately crashed the plane?" Marc demanded.

Sam could only nod. Then suddenly the words

started to pour out like water from a broken water main. He said that back in college Garrett had been involved in one of those college fun stunts that had backfired. Sam had gone along with it at first, then couldn't back out. And after it was over he lived in fear that one day someone would find out about his involvement. Garrett knew that, and had held it over him ever since.

"That's why you let him get away with it?" Marc asked. "He was blackmailing you?"

Sam nodded again. "Garrett's smart," he said. "Brilliant. And the way he had it planned, I guess I thought. . . ." His voice trailed off.

For almost a minute, no one said a word. The only sound was crickets in the brush, and the occasional soft hoot of an owl on the hunt.

"You knew what Garrett was going to do at Preston?" one of the officers asked.

Sam looked up. "No. That I didn't know. I knew he worked for them. I knew he had done something and he was planning an elaborate escape scheme. That's all." He swallowed hard. "He said I'd never see him again or hear from him."

The two state troopers eyed each other briefly. "OK," one of the officers said at last. "We'll want to talk to you about that some more," he told Sam. "Later."

Sam sighed. "I'll be around," he said softly. "I've got a few loose ends to pull together." He looked at Marc as the police officers left. His meaning was clear. His gaze moved across to Rick. "I guess I've got a few things to learn."

Marc punched his cousin lightly on the shoulder. "Maybe we both have something to learn," he put in gently. "I thought I had this business of being a Christian all figured out—until I met Rick, here. And his uncle. For them it's something real."

Sam Blair's eyes dropped. "I'm not a very good actor, am I?"

Rick smiled and nodded his encouragement. Marc had made a good start. And it looked like maybe Sam had taken a step in the right direction, too.

"I guess we all have something to learn," he said. "About living instead of acting."

Rick placed the lens cap back on his camera. Maybe those routine assignments from Starr News weren't so bad after all.